Stahlgewitter

at the gates of

Moscow

-

Waffen SS

in Combat

a German view of WW2

Operation Barbarossa 1941

through German eyes

written by
friedrich von Gatow

"Only the dead have seen the end of war."

Plato

This book is based on true events, parts of the story are fabricated. Some names and identifying details have been changed to protect the privacy of individuals as long they are no historic persons.

This book is dedicated to the fallen soldiers of World War II. These men shouldn't be forgotten. We need to always be vigilant so the sacrifices they made were not in vain. They swore a holy oak and did their duty. Their death should be a warning to the living to keep the peace in future!

SS-Brigadeführer der Waffen-SS Otto Kumm
(Brigadier General)
Commander of SS-Regiment „Der Führer"

* 1 October 1909 Hamburg † 23 March 2004 Offenburg

Road to Moscow – German forces of the Wehrmacht
on their way to soviet capital

Soldiers of the Waffen-SS Regiment "Der Führer"
fighting against general winter and the soviets!

Military Situation

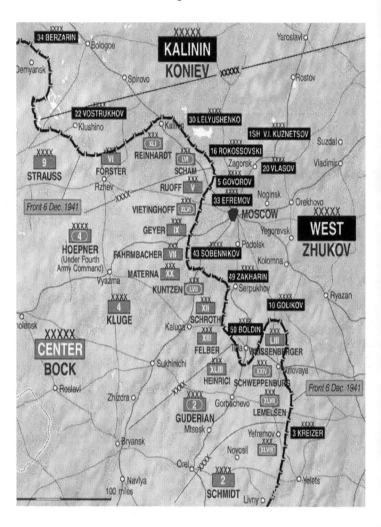

The Frontline at the gates of Moscow around the 6th of December 1941

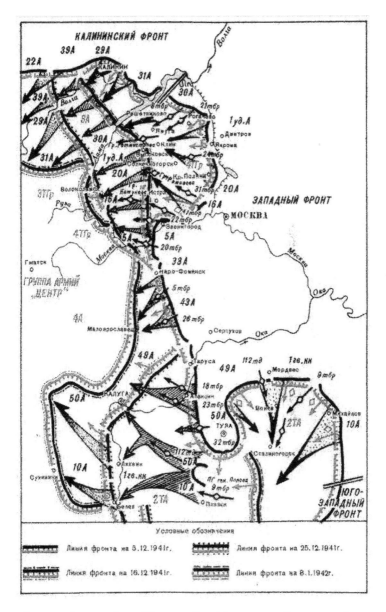

Original soviet military situation map from counter operations between December 5th 1941 and January 8th 1942 The Germans was able to hold their line!

Prologue

The German Army Group Center achieved an overwhelming tactical victory during the twin battles of Bryansk and Vyazma during the first half of October 1941. It remained to be seen during the following weeks if it could be expanded operatively and bring forth the crowning result of Moscow's capture. The impact it left upon the Russians was great at any rate. The Soviet government was moved to Kuibyshev; great masses of the population left the city, but Stalin remained. The city's inhabitants who had remained and were able to perform manual labor began to construct defensives in the city's suburbs.

Looting followed-up, and on crude, quickly made leaflets stood the phrase Death to the communists! The hungry people stood in long lines before the bread stores and grumbled, "Stop this war, make an end!" A.M. Samsonov wrote in his book The Great Battle before Moscow: A mood of dismay had spread throughout the city. The evacuation of the industrial operations, ministries, and institutions were accelerated. Signs of confusion amongst the population surfaced during this time. There were individuals who spread panic, abandoned their work places and hastened to get out of the city. There were traitors too, who took advantage of the situation, stole socialist property and who attempted to undermine the soviet state. The official announcements from the soviet government sounded very serious. From the Kremlin, Stalin attempted everything possible to have England initiate speedy efforts of relief. General Zhukov was given the responsibility to defend the threatened city. Then suddenly, and especially early during this year, the winter came and along with it terrible cold temperatures. German operations ended abruptly. The engines and even automatic weapons froze-up. In no way were their uniforms sufficient in these biting cold temperatures, which went as far down as minus forty-five degrees Celsius. Masses of the inadequately equipped troops suffered serious frostbite. Nevertheless, the troops fought their way forward through ice and masses of snow with incredible tenacity.

However, the weeks of fighting that the Balkan campaign had cost were not to be recovered. The original German intention was to have only portions of the eastern forces remaining in Russia. It had been planned that after the destruction of the soviet forces, a weak contingent of troops were to be left stationed there, and that it would suffice to have them distributed at important geographic locations throughout the land. The masses of German troops would have been pulled back to acceptable accommodations; as long as no other far reaching plans were being contemplated. It came to pass differently. The German eastern forces, with every division thrown into action, were now involved in serious combat, exposed to the hard Russian winter, far away from home. The German supply system could not operate very efficiently, and their capacity

13

efforts were yet further hindered by the ever increasing partisan activity. Appropriate clothing, which were field-tested and found to be sufficient for the Russian winter, were not yet available. Only the Luftwaffe and the Waffen-SS were to some extent better prepared. Wool collecting efforts, which were initiated immediately, showed the enthusiastic generosity of the German population. But weeks would pass before the items would reach the fronts. Naturally, the suitability of the donated clothing for the soldiers was marginal. Other types of equipment and weapons too were, at times, not adequate for winter-warfare in Russia.

All this resulted in a reduction of the German tactical and fighting superiority to that of inferiority, in face of an opponent who was accustomed to, much better equipped for, and had weapons that were superiorly attuned to, the winter climate. The soviet leaders seemed to have waited just for this most favorable event, were the German attacking strength would be exhausted and were the climatic conditions would allow them to play- out their trumps.

Stahlgewitter at the gates of Moscow

The 3rd Battalion of the Regiment "Der Führer" (DF), or rather what was left of it, had captured a large factory in the western outskirts of Lenino. Tenaciously, the companies, which were nothing more than platoon sized, fought their way through town, past the train station, and onward to the eastern outskirts, where they took-up positions. Thus a satellite town of Moscow, which is only seventeen kilometers from the capital's outskirts away, was in the hands of the Regiment DF. Untersturmführer (Lieutenant) Paul Hessler has occupied a number of ruins in the outskirts of Lenino with his company, which numbered 38 men.

The weakest squad in his company was led by Unterscharführer (corporal) Helmut Kolbe; there were only seven men, but yet they still had two MG 2) crews. A Sturmgeschütz (assault gun) had taken-up position within some ruins and stood lurking. A second one was over with the neighboring left- flanking company. The frontline, which the company must hold, was around three hundred meters long. The soldiers, all of which were young volunteers, had entrenched themselves amongst the ruins with distances of around ten to twelve meters apart. It was impossible to dig fox-holes in these temperatures, which was minus thirty degrees. Except for minor force-reconnaissance activity, there were no attacks to be feared at night. This was why only a skeleton crew remained in position after nightfall and that stayed until dawn. Whoever didn't have sentry duty went into a cellar that served the squad as sleeping quarters and a place to warm up in. How did such a cellar hole look like? There was a trapdoor, located in the hallway of the house, through which one gained access to the cellar by way of a rickety ladder. In one corner of the room the soldiers had set-up a fireplace, which was fed by the scorched wood from the ruins above. Due to excessive smoke, they stoked it only so much to merely let the coals glow. To let the smoke escape and for fresh air to get in, the trapdoor always remained open. On the other side of the room there was a pile of potatoes, which was bitterly fought over by rats and mice.

When the rodents got too carried away with their fighting, one of the soldiers would take a spade and throw a smoldering piece of wood at them. Then they'd have it quiet again for a while. The men's bedding consisted of small twigs, straw, tent-halves and coats. If all was quiet for a little while, the place almost seemed homey. The fire's glow spread a dull shadowy light, and in its luminosity the men's faces looked as if they were sitting in hell. Every once in a while, one of the wood pieces would snap or crackle and sent a small spurt of sparks flying. Sturmmann (private 1st class) Kurt Grossert squatted by the fire and poked the coals with his bayonet. "Anything done yet, Kurt?" asked the second MG-gunner (MG gunner II – assistant machine gunner) Eugen Baumann with his pleasant bass voice from the dark end of the room. "Nine potatoes and four strips of bacon, but I'm going to take them up to the men on watch, so that they get nice and warm around their hearts. You can continue to roast in the meantime, Eugen." Grossert put the bacon and potatoes into a mess tin, put on his coat, white camouflage shirt, gear, hung a captured Russian MP3) around his neck, and then scrambled up the old and weak ladder. This old ladder won't last for long, Kolbe thought, it should be fixed; otherwise it could be catastrophic if it should break during an alert. "Have you greased your nose sufficiently?" Kolbe called after Grossert. "I've already smeared plenty of lard on my honker, Herr Unterscharführer!" They still had plenty of lard from fallen Russian soldier's rucksacks and machorka tobacco, but bread was fast running low.

Ammunition for the rifles and machine guns were also running out. They had to make use of captured stock. The supply system wasn't working proper, because the supply lines were too rough and far too long. As Grossert exited the cellar hole, the icy north-easterly wind attacked him like a beast. It was certainly at least minus forty. He felt it in his nostril openings, when they froze together. Quickly, he pulled the hood over his nose and mouth. Sometimes the clouds were torn apart by the wind, allowing the moon's sickle and stars to shine upon the snowy landscape, as if they wanted to see if those odd beings down below hadn't yet stopped with their nonsense. They have not; they still lurk at each other with their fingers resting against the triggers of their murderous weapons. Grossert went to the first machine gun emplacement. Sturmmann

Otto Schmidt and Schütze (private) Heinrich Hofer occupied the position. They both cowered behind some low remains of a wall, wrapped-up in coats and shelter-halves. They had created a solid machine gun nest by using the surrounding stone rubble and wood pieces. From here, they had a field of fire that reached to about three hundred meters, over almost featureless terrain. Beyond that there was a small forest, where the main road and railroad line to Moscow went through. Schmidt, the first MG gunner, had wrapped an old woolen shawl around the weapon's receiver to prevent it from freezing-up. One of them was awake, while the other soldier tried to sleep, as far as was possible in this cold.

Hofer stared over to the enemy, who had positions along the forest's boundary. According to statements given by prisoners, they were well laid-out bunker defenses, which had been placed along both sides of the road and railroad lines, leading to Moscow. The soldiers there were fresh troops from Siberia and Manchuria. The Siberians shot a flare into the air every once in a while, which could be seen floating down on their little parachutes and which flooded the combat zone with a pale light, until they went out in the snow. Grossert pulled out a mess tin from his coat. "Here, take some before it gets cold. Is anything unusual going on?" "Tank engines rumbling once in a while. They're keeping the engines warm, so they don't freeze-up. That's all," Hofer said. Grossert stomped to the left over to another emplacement where Kollaritsch-Johann and the

Swede, Ole Johannsen, were and cursed under his breath, because he almost tripped and fell. It was not far to over there. The snow crunched under his boots. He was glad that he had found a dead Siberian, whose feet were as large as his, and who's Walnikis (felt boots) he was wearing now. His other comrades were already equipped with these boots. It'd be nice to also have a fur cap. Well – maybe tomorrow evening! The Russian sub-machinegun, which many Landsers had made acquaintance with, was an excellent weapon that could be dependent on. It functioned even in extreme cold temperatures. If only the lack of ammo for this weapon would not be.

One could depend only on captured ammunition, because such small caliber cartridges in the size 7.92 x 33 were not (yet) available to the German Wehrmacht. Kollaritsch and Johannsen were cowering by some destroyed timberwork. They both first rubbed-in bacon grease onto their noses, foreheads and chins. Then they devoured the warm potatoes and ate with relish the thick slices of bacon. "What's up?" asked Grossert. "Nothing, except the sounds of tank engines once in a while!" Kollaritsch answered. Unexpectedly, engine noise could be heard coming from within the town. Those must be their own Kübelwagen. They knew this sound. "Could it be that they're bringing us supplies and ammo?" wondered Johannsen. "Then I must go and have a look!" said Grossert, and then he trotted away. It was the Spieß (First Sergeant), Stabsscharführer Lauterbach, who rumbled down the main street with two Kübelwagen. Grossert ran towards the vehicles while waving his arms. "Halt!" he called out, "halt -- or do you want to go all the way over to the Ivan4)?" The vehicles came to a stop. The first sergeant asked; "Where is Untersturmführer Hessler's command post?" "Here you are absolutely in the right place, Stabsscharführer. Take your vehicle close to the gable side of that house, because the Ivan will soon make his presence felt!" The vehicles had barely reached the prescribed cover, when the screams of the rocket projectiles, which the Russians lovingly call Katjusha, approached with jets of flames trailing behind them in the dark of the night. Not far where the vehicles had previously stood, a volley crashed into the area with flashes and thunderous sound.

Untersturmführer Hessler and his company messenger appeared from out of the dark of the night. "Nice that you've made it through again," he said. "You are long-awaited -- I hope you don't bring us frozen linseed stew!" "No, Untersturmführer, no stew; plenty of rations and ammunition," Stabscharführer Lauterbach reported. "Watch out!" Grossert called out. "The next volley is on its way!" Screaming, a dozen fiery rocket tails arced their way over the German lines towards the factory that lies in the western edge of town. "The usual harassing fire, when there's movement by us!" Hessler said and turned to the Stabsscharführer: "Bring everything over into the second house from here. The command post is there." Facing his messenger and Grossert: "Kirchner, you notify the squads to come and receive food and ammunition. Grossert, you go and let your squad leader know!" Suddenly, a heavily laden figure approached Untersturmführer Hessler. Sturmmann Mikosch reporting back for duty, Untersturmführer!" Out of happiness, Hessler grabbed Mikosch by his arm. "Man, Mikosch! It is nice that you're here. Is your arm really all right? It looked pretty bad -- the wound..." Grossert, who had stared at Mikosch like some world wonder, could no longer hold himself back. Interrupting the company commander, he blurted out, "Hey Franzl! You're coming with us right away -- or?" Hessler grinned as the two comrades gave each other a hug. "Go ahead with them, Mikosch. Your squad comrades will be happy.

I'll drop by later for a welcoming drink!" Mikosch was the first to go down into the cellar. "I'm back, buddies!" he said with some emotion as he looked at the withered and frostmarked faces. With open mouths, they stared at the newcomer, who stood there in the dim light of the low fire, packedup in a lamb-fur coat, white snowshirt, and new felt boots. He stared back with a bit of embarrassment. "Jesus, Mikosch!" Unterscharführer Kolbe let out with great surprise. "You comin' directly from Vienna ... Hotel Sacher and such ..." Baumann-Eugen yelled, Franzl, are you nuts, you jerk ... What are you doing back here in this cold?" "I promised everyone that I'd be back in time for Moscow's capture. Henry Hendrick and Heinz Meyer came with me too. They had to remain in the rear for the time being, because there wasn't enough room in the vehicles ..." Kollaritsch interrupted him. "Unterscharführer," he said to Kolbe, "two men are supposed to get rations and ammo." "Go do that with Eugen. Franzl will stay with me." The distribution of the rations and the ammunition was accomplished before midnight. The supply people were in a hurry, because they had to go back and deploy behind the Istra before dawn. With a bottle of corn schnapps in hand, the company commander went into the cellar where Kolbe's squad was quartered. The Unterscharführer, together with Baumann, Grossert, and Mikosch, were squatting around the fire. The steam from the hot canned meat rose out of their mess kits, and lying beside the fire's hot embers were potatoes and bread. Hessler was invited to eat.

After they had eaten, everyone was allowed a big swallow from the bottle, and then Kolbe said, "It's time to relieve the others." Untersturmführer Hessler left the bottle of liquor there, wished the men a quiet night's watch, and then went out into the ice cold night. What a bunch of faithful fellows, he thought. They were so resolute in their effort to return to their units, to their comrades, many of whom were no longer here. They've fallen, froze to death, or were wounded. On this very day, Mikosch will have lice again. Tomorrow will be a hard day of fighting, were he may get killed. The four men that were relieved were sitting around the fire, cooked the canned meat in their mess kits, and roasted some potatoes and bread. Then they heard a meowing that sounded almost pleading. "A cat!"

exclaimed Hofer. "It feels the warmth, and it must be hungry too ... I'll go get it down." The cat was a black and white tomcat. It was a fine specimen, which started to hunt right away. In no time had he caught a fat rat and held it by its neck, which squeaked and wiggled in fear of death. Proud and with triumph he dragged it over to Kollaritsch, who grabbed a spade and beat the rat to death, and then kicked it into a far corner. The cat jumped after it with a mighty leap. Cozily, he ate it in the dark corner. "A smart critter!" Johannes determined. "Doesn't want to ruin our appetite." "We should call him Ivan," suggested Kollaritsch, "it must be one of those rowdies left- over from the Czar."

"Ivan the Terrible. He was Czar in the mid 1500s," the Swedish student, Ole Johannsen, explained to his comrades. "He expanded his territories and later-on, he persecuted his own subjects in a pathological manner." "Ole, why did you interrupt your studies on philosophy and German philology to come to us? Not out of sense of adventure?" Otto Schmidt wanted to know. "A little want for adventure is there. But that is not the actual reason. Soviet Russia's aggression against our neighbor, Finland, with whom we had friendly relations and have historic connections with, had touched me in a special way, as did Russia's occupation of Estonia, Latvia, Lithuania, and Bessarabia." Untersturmführer Hessler, who had inadvertently heard Johannsen's words, called down from the trap door, "Johannsen, you should become an officer. I will put in a request for you to attend a Junker school (officer candidate

school), with your concurrence." "Thank you, Untersturmführer! I request a short period to think
it over. Your offer honors me, but it comes a bit
hasty." The company commander wanted to say
something else, but didn't get a chance. Shots, fired
from a Russian MP, shrilled through the icy night;
excited shouts of alarm could be heard in between
the fire. "That was Kurt ... Grossert Kurt, Untersturmführer!" Schmidt exclaimed. Grab the weapons
and out! The Untersturmführer already hastened
ahead, with long strides. Schmidt and Hofer followed. It was only twenty meters to the MG nest,
where Kollaritsch and Baumann were on guard-
post. Hessler shot a flare, it whizzed into the air.

Shots fired from a Russian MP came from the
direction of the MG emplacement, and in-between
that the sounds of the MG-34 firing, which was
manned by Eugen Baumann. Pale light spread- out
as the flare went down. Now it was possible to see
a few figures working their way closer to the MG
nest by leaps and bounds, dressed in white camouflage suits and firing their MPs. From their stand-
point, which was on a large pile of rubble, Hessler,
Schmidt, and Hofer could recognize the Red Army
troopers very clearly. Kollaritsch and Johannsen
crawled closer forward. "Get down!" Hessler called
out – just a second later a fusillade of MP and
rifle fire was let loose, which forced the enemy to
take cover in the snow; they had approached the
MG nest to within fifteen meters. The Untersturmführer shot another flare, and as it sank lower,
spreading its light, Johannsen and Kollaritsch fired

their captured MPs while they charged at the Red Army soldiers, whom they had snuck up to from the side. None of the enemy escaped the hail of German bullets. One lightly wounded enemy soldier gave up after he had felt the ice cold barrel against his cheek as he pretended to be dead. "Go over to them and take away their submachine guns and rucksacks!" the Untersturmführer told Schmidt and Hofer. "But hurry, it's going to get hot again soon!" "Bring me a fur hat – a fairly large one!" Grossert called out after them. Six Red Army soldiers lie dead before the MG nest; the seventh had survived with merely a graze wound on his arm.

Yet he also dragged a few rucksacks into the cellar hole. Grossert got a fur hat that fit his head; he's very happy. Off with the cold steel helmet, on with the warm fur hat. In the mean time, flares had gone up over by the enemy too; the Russians were getting nervous. Every once in a while, a rifle shot would ring out. They waited to get the artillery into action; perhaps expecting the return of the force-reconnaissance team first. The prisoner and the captured equipment were brought to the company command post. A somewhat larger portion of the captured MPs, ammunition, bacon and machorka, went to Kolbe's squad. The enemy's artillery started to fire as the men were back inside their cellar and roasting bacon around the fire. Some of the shells had landed so close that chunks of frozen ground and iced snow tumbled into the cellar opening. Out of fear, the tomcat hid in the furthest corner of the potato pile. The artillery fire did not bother the four Landsers very much at all. They sat and enjoyed the roasted bacon and bread. Soon, at dawn, they would have to relief those on guard duty. The Red Army went into a counteroffensive with forces that had been brought from far away, to go against, for them, the more dangerous German Army Group Center on the 5 th of December 1941. The enemy's great and bloody counterstrike began by the German 36th Infantry Division (mot.)5), and spread from there along Army Group Center's 1000 kilometer front-lines. Along this line, the German offensives had, literally, been frozen stiff. Two mortar groups went into position behind Hessler's company just before dawn of the fifth and before the enemy artillery began its bombardment.

The Russian artillery fired relentlessly over the wide and snowy fields. The Landsers clenched their teeth as they pressed their bodies down into their cover; especially when the screeching rockets from the rocket launchers approached. The detonations burst open with eruptions of flying ice-chunks, pieces of frozen earth, snow and dirt fountains, and with a tornado of howling shrapnel and hissing powder gasses. Acidic smells permeated the air. Ever more, the white fields got inundated with dark spots. At times, a human body got torn to shreds, and then bloody body parts were thrown into the air and got smashed upon the snow. In the meantime it got light in the eastern horizon. Red skies death. A terrible howl suddenly approached Baumann and Grossert, crashed down closely right before them, to smash, with ear shattering noise, a fountain of stinking smoke into the air, which was accompanied by a spray of icy clumps of dirt and hot shrapnel. A swish of metal showered over the Landsers, who lie pressed down against the dirt. Baumann had his face pushed into the crook of his arm, half unconscious, gasped for air, and dug his mouth, nose, and chin into the cloth of his hood. He raised his head and saw a crater four steps before him, a meter wide and from which smoke was dissipating. His eyes watered from the searing slime. His skull was heavy and dazed. The stinking powder gasses moved over him. Grossert was not doing any better; he was half deaf after what seemed like an iron church tower bell rang against his eardrums.

The enemy's artillery fire was getting less. Only further to the rear, where the Sturmgeschütze and mortar crews were in position, did a few more volleys struck. With sighs of relief the men raised their heads. Those who were inside the cellars hurried to get out and, after they scurried in crouched manner, got to their positions. Now the young soldiers saw something that was not new to them anymore. The enemy attacked with a large force, much superior in numbers than they. Masses of them poured out of the forest. They bunched-up on top of tanks; clouds of snow got thrown into the air by the armored vehicles. It was a hair-raising sight for the forward observers as they saw the masses of attackers. Nevertheless, the soldier calmly passed-on the coordinates to his comrade manning the radio. Both had positioned themselves inside a half destroyed cottage. The self-propelled howitzers

began to fire at the enemy's tanks. Two Strumges-
chütze took the first T-34 under direct fire as it
approached along the street and was furthest advanced. One shell hit it between the turret and
chassis, the other shell glanced off. Then the hulk
stood on the street, smoking. The infantry sitting
on top of it got thrown off through the tank's
sudden stop, and then ran away from it. Just as
the tank commander opened a hatch a flame flashed
out with a thunderous roar. The tank had burst
apart from the explosions of its own ammunition.
Now it blocked the street for the other tanks. Yet
this did not bother the monsters, since the ground
was frozen rock-solid. Soon, another two tanks
stood burning in the snow.

In the meantime, the German mortars began to fire.
Round after round dropped amidst the attacking
ranks of the enemy. There were hundreds of them
and more and rolling in- between were the tanks,
thirty or more. A short time later, the own artillery fired over the heads of the Landsers, who
await the order to fire, and with thunderous sound
and bright flashes the shells detonated amongst the
rows of enemy troops. The detonation cascades stood
for short moments before they collapsed. The attackers threw themselves down, or got thrown down
by the shock waves or shrapnel. A few of the T-
34 had stopped and began firing high-explosive
shells into the ruins that stood at the edge of town.
The others continued their advance - and came into
the optics of the Sturmgeschütze. Soon, there were
eleven tanks lined-up before the German lines. The

Russian artillery began to fire at the German front lines again. Their infantry salso tarted to move forward at this time. Up until now, the Soviet attack was carried-out only haphazardly, but it suddenly began to gain momentum. The T-34s joined in on the preparing fire with high explosive shells and with their machineguns, as the infantry masses worked their way ever closer to the German lines. The tank engines roared and the snow got thrown into the air. They were coming! "Fire!" Now the men's pent-up tension was as if it were blownaway. They fired and the empty shells gathered in piles. The barrels soon turned hot.

A quick barrel-change on a MG – and then it continued to rattle garbs into the attackers, who were shocked by the amount of fire the received and dove for cover behind their tanks. But they were not completely safe there either; now another four tanks stood smoldering in the field. The attack began to falter. "Dawai!" The Soviet officers, sergeants and commissars drove the Siberian troops onward. The tanks fired what they could. The defenders too, were suffering high casualty rates. Three MG nests had been knocked-out by artillery and tank fire. The direct fire of the T-34s ceased. Their engines howled as they advanced again. Bullets from MPs and rifles zipped closely overhead as the Landsers peered over their cover to shoot back. Nevertheless, they fired all they could. Their blood raced through their arteries, like water gushing from a snow-melt. Their brains burnt. Their inner voices told them; shoot and hit or the enemy will get you instead! Either you or me! This is what the tankists6) were thinking too. Their tanks had come to within eighty meters of the German defensive lines. The fourteen tanks had only one Sturmgeschütz to worry about; the other one had been hit and incapacitated. Its crew was able to evacuate without harm, and joined their comrades on the lines. The one left-over Sturmgeschütz was forced to change its position continuously now. The men now knew what would come next; close quarter defense against the enemy tanks. They had taken measures for this beforehand. Geballte Ladungen7) and incendiary bottles lay waiting in the cellars. Two Landsers per cellar had gone to retrieve them.

The enemy tanks came closer with engines howling. Red Army troops, whose rows had been decimated by now, followed them while stooped over. The dead and wounded accumulated behind them. Untersturmführer Hessler, and together with Rottenführer (corporal) Kirchner, were prone behind a halffallen corner of a building waiting for the first tank. It had successfully broken through the defensive line. Hessler had two bundle charges and Kirchner two incendiary charges. With squeaking running-gear and rattling tracks, the dangerous foe swayed towards them. Schmidt kept the enemy infantry following the tank at bay with his MG. Baumann and Johannsen supported him effectively in this. Now the T-34 approached the remains of the house-corner, where Hessler and Kirchner were hiding. The tank stopped shortly, and then gave full throttle as if he wanted to knockdown the last remains of the wall. But suddenly, he veered off to the right. It seemed as if he had changed his mind. Or had he discovered Kollaritsch and Hofer in their MG nest? After the tank presented its rear quarter, Hessler and Kirchner jumped from behind the wall. Kirchner lit the gasoline-soaked cloth, which hung out from the bottle, and threw it on top of the tank's engine compartment; the vehicle stood about twenty meters away. Hessler pulled the fuse from the center grenade and threw it into the gasoline flames. Both men jumped behind a pile of rubble. A loud bang followed, after which the tank stopped and burned. Hessler and Kirchner leaped back behind the wall ruins and watched the burning tank from a hole.

Suddenly, the turret hatch flung open, a leather-helmeted head appeared and then quickly disappeared again after he had been hit by an MP garb, fired by Kirchner. The driver attempted to get out through another hatch, but got hit by a pistol-shot, fired by the Untersturmführer, and stayed slumped out of the opening. This was the end of the steel behemoth, which exploded with thunderous roar shortly thereafter. Then the next tank was hit. Baumann and Johannsen had knocked it out with incendiary and bundled charges. Baumann had scorched his right hand in the process. The Russian casualty rate was tremendous, and now there was no holding them back anymore; they fled. The rest of their tanks retreated too, going in high gear. Without concern, they rolled over their own dead and wounded comrades! Many of the fleeing men, especially the officers, got caught in a hail of fire and didn't make it back to their own lines. The Siberians failed to achieve even one successful breakthrough. Their mighty attack had been bloodily repulsed. Deceptive stillness befell the battle zone. The wounded had been brought into houses, which were still half-way intact, to be taken care of. One seriously wounded soldier had shot himself with a pistol. Kolbe's squad had survived with much luck and had suffered only one casualty; a lightly wounded man. Johann Kollaritsch had a shrapnel-wound in his right shoulder. Baumann barely felt the pain from the burn in his right hand, which he got while throwing the incendiary bottle. Other squads had suffered higher casualties. An unusual sort of silence had returned.

At noontime, the cloud cover dissipated some, allowing the sun to peer through open spots. Johannsen and Hofer returned to their cellar and were roasting bacon and potatoes. Hofer was melting some snow to get water. He wanted to brew some of the black tee that Mikosch had brought with from home. Ivan the cat was no longer in the cellar. Grossert assumed that he could get up the ladder, but not back down. "I hope they return with something to keep warm with," Baumann grumbled, "the damned cold is barely endurable. My whole body is cold, only my burnt hand is warm." Then he shouted, "I think I'm going to light myself on fire. Shitty, miserable war!" "This is the first time you said something like this," Otto Schmidt said. "I'm going to say this more often from now on. I have to let it out sooner or later. Damned, shitty, dirty, miserable war!" From out of the north, where the 10th Panzer Division was deployed, the sound of battle could be heard. This once proud division had only a few tanks left, maybe twenty or so. The DF Regiment, together with companies from this division, had achieved great successes. The Division Das Reich, which this regiment belonged to, and the 10th Panzer Division, were competing with each other who would be the first to get to the Red Square. Heinrich Hofer took-over the second MG. Machine gunners II and III were Franz Mikosch and Kurt Grossert. They were cowering inside their foxhole, slurping the hot tea. In between this, they ate the bacon and potatoes.

Ole Johannsen, who functioned as gunner III in Schmidt's machine gun crew, had been shot at by an enemy soldier with an MP while he brought warm food to the men. "I've already spotted the enemy soldier," said Schmidt. "He's over by the knocked-out tank." The other comrades, warned by the shots, had also spotted the enemy soldier, and were now more careful. The skies cleared-up in the afternoon and soon thereafter all hell broke loose. Soviet ground attack aircraft began their devil's dance with their on-board weapons and bombs. Over and over again they twisted and turned as they attacked. While new formations arrived, others pulled out, to be re-fueled and have ammo replenished. In between all this, Soviet fighters attacked to show what they were capable of. Prey was easy to spot with the good visibility. Like hawks they came down in a dive. The damaged Sturmgeschütz was an easy quarry. A mortar position was also taken under fire. The casualties among the infantry and in the MG emplacements were light, because their positions were attacked frontally. "Seems to be a day for the red air fleet," Untersturmführer Hessler declared to his company HQ platoon leader Kirchner. Sepp Kirchner, a farmer's boy from the Tyrolean Alps, was someone who spoke little. He simply grumbled, "Sure ..." Then he stuffed his pipe with machorka and left the undamaged room. The Untersturmführer didn't like the stink of machorka. He barely took a few puffs when he heard the sound of the Stalin organs. Artillery joined in. Angrily, he uttered, "Those assholes, them ..."

Shaking from cold and anxiety, the Landsers lingered inside their foxholes waiting for the enemy's attack, which must soon come. It should, if it was to be carried-out successfully before the onset of dusk. The Siberians attacked barely a half hour later with twelve T-34s. Immediately, the German artillery began to shoot a curtain of fire with good effect. The single Sturmgeschütz left its cover, despite the artillery barrage, to join in on the fight. The only surviving mortar crew also got themselves ready to fight. The enemy troops had already approached to within two hundred meters of the German lines when their artillery moved the fire further to the German rear. The attack was being carried-out with more force this time. The enemy soldiers must have got a serious scolding. Nevertheless, two tanks already stood destroyed in the fore field. The Sturmgeschütz shot one in flames, while a lucky shot from an anti-tank rifle demolished a track on the other tank. The rifleman, a Rottenführer from a neighboring platoon, had learned how to do it best: If he shot at the tank's armor, then he merely "knocked hello"; but if he fired at the tracks or bogey wheels, he might be successful to cause damage. If he were to succeed get a projectile inbetween the turret and chassis, then there might be a chance that the turret could not be turned anymore. Just as the attackers began advance up the flat rise towards the edge of town, the Sturmgeschütz destroyed a third tank. Now the German infantry weapons began to fire a fusillade of bullets. Like ragdolls some of the enemy soldiers fell off the tanks, others jumped off and pressed themselves into the snow.

The tanks went at it alone. With thunder and lightning a fourth tank blew-up. Now there were only eight T-26s left over, whose crewmen knew that the weak armor of their vehicles would be easy for the Germans to penetrate. They threw the gears into reverse. Two T-26s were destroyed by the Sturmgeschütz, and the other was put out of action by the antitank rifleman. While the tankists opened a hatch and attempted to escape, they were caught in an MG garb, and then dropped back inside. The enemy infantry also pulled back. This time they didn't go back from where they came from, inside the forest, but to just before the edge of the forest – to the German's surprise. There, they dug-in into the snow. Perhaps it was a type of punishment not to allow them to return into the woods. Their wounded comrades partially lie in masses before the German lines and whined pathetically. Not a single person helped them. The Germans knew from experience that wounded men's comrades were being kept from doing so by force of arms. The skies turned dark. The onset of night would bring snow with it. The guards inside the strong-points stared over to the enemy, who occasionally shot a flare into the air, which then floated slowly downward, flooding the combat zone in a hazy light until it went out in the snow. The moaning of the wounded enemy soldiers, still lying in the fore field, had almost subsided. Most of them may have shut their eyes forever by the merciful icy frost.

They too, had a mother, a wife, children, who were at home and whose thoughts were with the beloved son, husband, or father. Perhaps they prayed for him that he would come home soon well-up. The enemy shot harassing fire into the fore field. Sometimes, a shell would detonate here or there with a loud bang. It seemed as if they wanted to prevent the wounded men to be brought in by the Germans and to be interrogated. It began to snow. Unterscharführer Kolbe approached, accompanied by Kurt Grossert. "Anything new?" he asked in a low tone of voice. "Nothing unusual, Unterscharführer!" Hofer answered. "Well then, go back into the cellar. Come back in two hours again." While Grossert sat in the MG nest, Kolbe stood a little distance away behind a ruined wall and tensely peered out through a hole into the fore field. One had to be especially careful during snowfall, because noises were muffled by it. Kolbe stomped his feet in order to keep warm. A crust of ice had formed over a portion of his hood, which covered his mouth. His homeland lies in the Bohemian Erz Mountains. Snow lies there too during this time of the year. Right after the Anschluss, which united Sudetenland and Austria with Germany, he had volunteered to join this unit, which was composed mainly of Austrians and Germans of the Sudetenland. During the fall of 1938, he met Paul Hessler, his current company commander, in Graz who had been Sturmmann back then. The two had a friendly relationship since the war with Poland. Paul Hessler, who stemmed from Austria's Salzburgerland, was a first class comrade.

He was always there for his men, day and night, in private and officially too. "Well, Sepp, are your thoughts at home with St. Nicholas, or do you think the Krampus (helpers of St. Nicholas) are coming?" Untersturmführer Hessler had asked who suddenly stood by Kolbe. Kolbe shuttered for a fleeting moment. "If the red Krampus had snuck-up on me, I'd be finished now." "It may be possible that a few of them could appear in this snowfall," Hessler admitted, and then added, "We received a 5 cm Pak 8) to reinforce our positions, and they brought a sack full of mail for our battalion." "Just in time for Nicholas gifts." Kolbe felt glad. Mail-call was like a holiday for the men. Mail from the parents, girlfriends, relatives, or friends, brought with them a bit of warmth and brightness to this cold and gloomy loneliness ... The temperatures had dropped down to minus 45 to 50 degrees centigrade; its icy grip had a hold on humans, animals, weapons and motors. No man could stay out longer than an hour in his snowy hole; unless, he had the appropriate clothing on. The soldiers put on whatever they could. That caused them to become ungainly and helped little to keep warm. Since it was not possible to get washed thoroughly, the men's clothing became a breeding ground for lice, which ate their way into the skin. Bad diarrhea was caused by the rations, which got to the men frozen solid. Butter had to be sucked - like candy, and bread had to be hacked into edible pieces. The companies shrunk ever more. There were more casualties through frostbite and diseases of the intestinal tract than through combat wounds.

In the early morning hours, a loud bang sounded out; it came from the left neighboring company. An enemy raiding-patrol had taken advantage of the heavy snowfall and attempted to take-out a position. However, the experienced Siberians had went against well-equipped German troops, who threw them back with MG and MP fire and with hand grenades. Shortly after that, the snowfall stopped, the clouds dissipated and a blue sky appeared. In this clear weather, the soldiers were able to see the towers of Moscow even without binoculars. A German 10 cm gun battery fired harassment fire into the city. The soviets fired back with Stalin organs and a battery of howitzers. It achieved no success, so it re- directed its fire on the German lines and increased until it was a real barrage. The positions of the 1 st and 3rd Battalions were inundated with thunderous detonation flashes, smoke, snow, and dirt geysers. German artillery positions were attacked by Soviet ground attack aircraft with anti-personnel bombs. Puffs of explosions from the German light Flak 9) hovered in the azure blue skies. They were able to shoot a few of the combat planes down and to chase the others away. down and to chase the others away. Strong infantry units, supported by tanks, now attacked. The German artillery seemed to have been largely spared by the air attacks, because they put out an effective curtain of fire. The Russians seemed to be attempting a breakthrough in a larger scale, because their tanks were equipped with additional fuel tanks. Despite the effective German fire, the attackers came closer.

It was possible to hear a little of the infantry's battle cries between the general combat noise. The Landsers listened-up: some of the voices seemed to be coming from very young people. The gaps that the German artillery caused in the attacking enemy ranks were continuously being filled back up. They seemed to have an endless supply of soldiers. With motionless eyes, the Germans stared at the scenery before them. Their trigger fingers, the only finger which extended out individually from the mittens, touched the triggers of their weapons. The enemy had not yet approached to within effective range. The closer they got, the more they bunched up. They were scared, and this was why they bunched-up like sheep in a thunderstorm. Untersturmführer Hessler, together with Kirchner, was lying close to Sepp Kolbe. It must be a miracle that he was still amongst the living. He was always up front. His eyes sat inside deep caverns and his cheeks were shrunken. A young man with an old face! It was marked by exhaustion, cold, the hardness and the horrors of war. "Fire!" With a sudden wallop the German fire opened up. The attackers dropped to take cover, while others crowded behind the tanks, which were under fire by the Sturmgeschütz and Pak. From those T-34s that had advanced the furthest, two had already been disabled and were standing in the battlefield smoldering. None of the following T-26s had yet been hit. "Shoot the fuel tanks!" the Untersturmführer shouted. This was not easy.

The fuel tanks, which were mounted in the rear and behind the turrets, must be shot at an angle, and this was difficult to do from their standpoints. But shrapnel from the mortars had caused three of them to burst into flames. Their onboard ammo exploded with mighty bursts, flares went flying in different directions, and oily smoke rose into the sunny sky. One T-34 got hit in its running gear, which caused it to turn around its own axis. The hatches opened-up and the crew attempted to escape, but they got hit by MG garbs and thus fall back inside. The tank commander hung out of the hatch and over the side of the turret and was soon engulfed in flames; it was a morbid thing to see. Untersturmführer Hessler, followed by Kirchner, crawled towards a wall. He looked for and found a spot, which offered him a good field of fire. He fired a long burst from his MP – it caused a fuel tank to burst into flames. In no time, the whole tank had turned into a torch. The Russians ended their attack and pulled back again. Now their ground attack planes came into play again. The Germans cursed. "Darn it, where is our Luftwaffe!" Although the planes had caused relatively little damage, they still forced the Germans to keep down, which prevented them to effectively fight the newly attacking enemy infantry. As the enemy air force flew off, they could look and see that the enemy tanks had got rid of the fuel tanks. All the courage the youthful soldiers and the Siberians might muster couldn't make a difference. With bloody losses, they were once again repulsed.

However, it did not take long before they returned, after their artillery had put-out another preparing fire. Repeatedly their troops charged against the German lines to achieve the all-important breakthrough so important for their offensive but were repulsed each time. As darkness fell over the land, the enemy ceased all further attacks. The German soldiers breathed a sigh of relief. "That was a close one again!" Kolbe said to Hessler, while taking in a deep breath "A few of the young ones had come to within fifteen, twenty meters. Spirited fellows they are!" "You can say that again. We must get a hold of one of them." Hessler, Kolbe, and Kirchner listened-up all of a sudden. Not too far away a young voice whined in a low tone: "Oh boshe moj ... oh, maminka "He said: Oh, my God Oh my mother," Kolbe translated, since he understood a little Russian. While Kolbe and Kirchner provided cover, Hessler crawled carefully to the moaning Red Army soldier, who lay amidst a group of fallen men. He took a close look at the wounded man, since this is what he assumed to have before him, but then he discovered that it was a young woman. "Jesus – that is a girl!" As the komsomol member heard German As the komsomol member heard German words, she attempted to raise herself up. Horrified, she stared at Hessler and searched for words. Saying kind words to her and with a soothing tone of voice, he gently pushed her back down. He quietly called for his two comrades to come over. "Carry her to the command post and check her wounds. Seems to be the lower calf." The Russian girl moaned with pain.

Kirchner, who carried her by the lags, cursed over the blood running over the sleeve of his white camouflage shirt. A scattering of artillery shells fell as harassment fire within the German lines. Different flares whizzed up into the star filled night sky. Ole Johannsen and Kurt Grossert sat in their cellar hole and were attempting to get the fire going again. The tomcat sat close by and watched them with interest. Ole went to go up and get fire wood, while Kurt hacked bacon and bread into usable sizes. Johannsen threw down some wood and then got a few mess tins filled with snow. He sat the tins onto the fire, which was burning again. Tee time just before midnight. "Hey, Ole," Grossert said. "You have a calendar inside your head. Is Nicholas Day today or tomorrow?" Johannsen thought for a moment before he answered, "Today."

Kolbe had sent the two men into the cellar, because both had received minor injuries during the day's battle. Grossert had a grazing shot wound over his left forehead and Johannsen a grazing shot wound on his upper arm. They helped each other with their bandages. It would not be so bad if it weren't for those damned lice, those blood-thirsty creatures! After they had eaten and drank, they went to relief Eugen Baumann and Franz Mikosch. Squad leader Helmut Kolbe, who constantly patrolled between the MG positions, went down into the cellar once in a while to get warmed-up. It had been especially cold during this night with the clear sky. This meant relieving the men who were on watch every hour. Baumann asked, Unterscharführer, what is the matter with our Luftwaffe?

Why don't they fly missions anymore?" "They'll return sometime. Maybe they're needed more elsewhere." During the commander's inspection rounds, he told the men that the offensive against Moscow had been called off. The men brooded over this news. For what reason was it called off? The hard winter? Was it the effectively fighting Siberian divisions, who were well equipped with weapons, winter clothing and white camouflage? They most certainly played a role, but not the deciding one. During local counterattacks, even they had to relent to the weakened companies of the regiment. After the betrayal of Stalin's master spy, Dr. Sorge, concerning Japan's secret pact, that they would not get involved with the war against the Soviet Union,

Stalin was relieved. The incubus that Japanese divisions would march into Siberia from Manchuria had been taken away. Stalin knew that he did not have to fear a two-front war anymore, so now he could order his Siberian rifle divisions, which were among his elite divisions, to be speedily transported from the Far East to the western front. Only training units remained in Siberia. Or was the reason for the end of the offensive due to failed planning on part of the Oberkommando der Wehrmacht (OKW – Wehrmacht Supreme Command), the Führerhauptquartier (Hitler's military headquarter), and the general staff? Had the Red Army's strength been underestimated? Was it due to the Luftwaffe's inability to stop or disturb sufficiently the enemy's supply columns to the front even east of Moscow?

Moscow had been bombed thirty five times between the 4th of October to the 5th of December 1941. The season of mud during fall, the hard winter, the constant re-deployments, and the difficulties of supplying the troops sufficiently, led to a drop of combat effectiveness amongst the units. So much so that it was not possible to fly much anymore. It became the duty of the troops to make do with what they had during this crisis. It may have been due to the poor system of roadways and railways within the conquered territories. There may have been many reasons to be argued. One thing was for certain; the German combat divisions gave their best. They performed beyond the call of duty. The Divisions Das Reich, the 10th Panzer Division and those from the XXXX Panzercorps, had suffered

7582 casualties from all ranks from the 9th of October to the 5 th of December, 1941. The casualties suffered along the entire eastern front up to the 5 th of December, 1941, were 750,000 soldiers. Just before mid-night, as Baumann and Mikosch wanted to relief Otto Schmidt and Heinrich Hofer, the mail was handed out. Receiving mail was like a festive day for the soldiers. It possessed something like a celebratory aspect – a jovial occasion. News – from home, from the loved ones! Their thoughts meandered to where home was, so far away. Baumann had tears in his eyes as he read the letter from his parents. Schmidt looked up and asked him what the matter was. Baumann waved him off and said it was nothing. It is a tiny piece of home he was holding in his hands.

Otto Schmidt felt this too, as he read his mother's words. "... and come home soon, safe and sound, my boy. We miss you much ..." He too, wiped away tears. During the night of the 6th of December, going on the 7th, Unterscharführer Kolbe, along with Rottenführer Kirchner and Sturmmann Anholzer, went out into the fore field to do reconnaissance. It had become cloudy again after midnight and then it started to snow. While ducking, the three men snuck around corpses covered with snow. The sharp eyes of Kolbe and Kirchner looked at the grotesquely shaped and frozen human bodies lying in the snow, while Anholzer provided cover. The two men searched the rucksacks to see if there was any submachine gun ammo in them. They stuffed the drum magazines into a sack as they find them. Bacon and sunflower seeds too, were collected. Whenever a flare went up, they threw themselves down and pretended to be dead. Near a tank wreck, they found a dead medic, whose backpack contained a bunch of bandages and all sorts of other items. After they had gathered enough material, Kirchner shouldered the sack, while Kolbe and Anholzer slung Russian submachine guns over their shoulders, and then they made their way back to the own lines. The wounded Russian woman lay in a cellar, which was the company command post, and moaned with pain. Sitting beside her, lit by the feeble light of a petroleum lamp, was an old Babushka (Grand- mother) giving her words of comfort. Kirchner searched the Rucksack for any painkiller.

He showed the old lady different types of little boxes, tins, and bottles. She pointed at a bottle, filled with pills, and put up two fingers. Kirchner got some bandages ready and then made the ba- bushka understand for her to change the bandages. She nodded affably. "Da – da." "Spasibo (thanks)!" the komsomol member said silently, and then she spoke with the toothless old woman. Except for weak harassing fire, the night remained relatively quiet. It had stopped snowing just before dawn. The clouds had dissipated, revealing a wonderful blue sky. There seemed to be something going on in the south-west. A heavy barrage could be heard from there. There, integrated with the 7th Infantry Di- vision was the French Voluntary Legion Regiment no. 638. Its commander, Colonel Labonne, used to be a military attaché in Turkey. The weather was clear and the towers of Moscow could be easily seen again. Unterscharführer Kolbe had just nodded-off beside the fireplace, when he registered loud sounding aircraft engines. The own air force had arrived, with Stukas10) and Me-109s! He rose quickly, grabbed his MP and hurried up the ladder. Flares rose all along the German lines: Here we are! The swarms of Stukas, accompanied by the fighters, flew off towards the forest. Then the usual scenery unfolded before the men's eyes. One plane after another dove down, some almost vertically, with sirens howling. They attacked the enemy bunker positions and artillery batteries. The ground quaked. High towers of smoke rose from within the forest. The on-board cannon of the Me-109s fired in between all this, hunting trucks and infantry positions. The men cheered.

Finally, they were back, the black Hussars of the air! "Will we attack again?" Kolbe asked Untersturmführer Hessler. "No, Sepp, quite the contrary. Tonight we will retreat towards the Istra River. There's supposed to be a strong-point type of defensive system there, built by the Pionieren (combat engineers)" "Who will remain to cover the retreat?" "Our battalion and one from the Regiment Deutschland (Germany) will keep contact with the enemy." When the young men heard this piece of news, the enthusiasm they had possessed since the first few months of the eastern campaign went away for good, and moral sunk down to nothing. But they still maintained their iron stoicism. Shortly after dark, the Spieß (first sergeant) and his driver came and brought cold rations and ammunition to the front lines. Sitting in the second Kübelwagen were six men, who'd been wounded during the first weeks of the eastern campaign, and who were now sound enough to return to the company. Among the six were Henry Hendrick, who'd been wounded on the 20th of July, and Heinz Meyer, both were members of Kolbe's squad. With them two, the squad had a total strength of nine men now, which, when one considered the company's overall strength of thirty two men, was a lot. The newcomers were dressed in proper winter clothing and were also in good spirits. However, when they learned that they would retreat during this night, their moral dropped too.

The Flemish Henry Hendrick had brought with him a bottle of Genever from home, which must be enjoyed "drop-by-drop". Heinz Meyer had ten wristlets along, which had been knitted by the women from his hometown, with "the best wishes and greetings". The comrades were touched. They were The comrades were touched. They were happy that the people back home were thinking about them. When Heinz Meyer told them that even young and pretty girls were involved in the knitting, they were all the more happy. St. Nicholas day had arrived to them after all. Just before mid-night, the Division Das Reich had initiated its retreat. The 3rd Battalion covering the retreat had a remaining strength equal to a company. Now it had to occupy a too-large portion of the defensive lines. It was a difficult task for the battalion and its commander,

Hauptsturmführer (captain) Kempin. The 2nd Battalion did not exist anymore; the remains of which had been distributed among the 1 st and the 3rd Battalions. The combat engineers were still busy in the fore field putting-out land mines in particularly exposed sections. Light harassment fire from the enemy was spread along the front lines. It began to snow at mid-night and the hard frost had relented some. It was still minus thirty degrees, however. Double sentries patrolled between the MG positions, which were spread far apart. The snowfall became heavy after mid-night. Now it was difficult for the sentries to maintain the correct direction between the strong points. Kolbe and Grossert took off boards from a fence to mark the pathway between the positions by sticking then into the snow.

This simplified the orientation a lot. The Sturmgeschütz, the 5 cm Pak and the mortar group were still present. They were to go back just before the rear guard was to do so. After mid-night, a Siberian reconnaissance troop on skis advanced along the railway. The platoon sized unit got trapped inside a mine field and was taken under fire by Schmidt's MG, which was located nearby. The Siberians were almost completely decimated. Only a few of the Red Army troopers were able to escape. Shortly thereafter, the Pak and the mortar men retreated. The Sturmgeschütz wanted to retreat together with the rear guard to the new defensive lines, which lay behind Ivanovskoje. They had to be taken back this far due to enemy breakthroughs to the north and south. It was not far away, maybe ten or twelve kilometers. Sometime later, the rear guard began to retreat. Rottenführer Kirchner and Sturmmann Anholzer said good-bye to the old Russian woman, which sat beside the wounded komsomol member. "Take care, babushka, and thanks a lot for the kartoshki!" He looked at the wounded girl, who looked at him with fearful eyes. He made it clear to her that she would soon be with her companions again. "Germanski njet Moscva!" he told her. She understood. Her eyes filled with tears. "Spasibo," she spoke softly. "Sdrastwudje (good day)!" The old lady made the sign of the cross and said, "Do swidaniya (good bye)!" The last to pull back was Kolbe's squad. Grossert poured a bucket of snow onto the fire and said to the tomcat, "You'll have it warm again soon, when your comrades return.

Later, Ivan." Despite the utmost care to keep the withdrawal secrete, the Russians must've noticed something, because they pushed forward immediately afterwards. Brandner and his squad were just leaving the western part of Lenino when MG fire could be heard in the eastern part. What does this mean? The men wondered. There's no one left of us in town. What are they shooting at? Orientation in the heavy snowfall was possible only by poles, which were stuck along the roadway. The other comrades and the Sturmgeschütz were already several hundred meters ahead. Unterscharführer Kolbe and Sturmmann Grossert were the last men of the squad. They kept turning around to look back into the darkness and the snowflakes, listening ... nothing there. A while later Kolbe noticed a shuffling noise that seemed familiar to him. "Someone is coming on skis, Kurt. Get your MP ready!" he said to Grossert silently and with excitement in his voice. As soon as the noise was close enough, Kolbe and Grossert opened fire with their captured Russian submachine guns. The enemy didn't fire a single shot; only cries of pain could be heard. But suddenly, an MP garb roared up very close- by and sent bullets between the two men, zipping past their ears. They threw themselves into the snow as fast as lightning and returned the fire. Grossert threw an egg hand grenade. It flashed and boomed and then it was silent. Otto Schmidt came and had positioned himself behind the two with his machine gun.

"Get the hell away from here!" Brander called over to them. They got up and ran until they met up with the squad again. The company messenger, sent by the commander, had arrived by the squad in the meantime to find out what the shooting was all about. "Anderl," Kolbe said. "Go tell the Untersturmführer to watch the flanks, because Siberians could appear on skis. They're already inside Lenino." There was not another firefight. Just before dawn they arrived in their new positions, which ran along the edge of a forest. There were bunkers, which had been blown out of the frozen ground and made with logs and covered with roofing felt and clods of dirt. Each bunker had room for five men. The walls and the flooring were made of logs and wooden boards. The smell of wood did well. The actual fighting emplacements were without roofs. The Pioniers even built a sauna within the forest, and the field kitchen was there too, located more towards the rear. The soldiers received barley stew with beef right after their arrival, served in insulated containers. Kolbe's group sat around inside their bunker. Only four were outside at the MG positions, keeping watch. It was Otto Schmidt with Heinz Meyer and Heinrich Hofer with Henry Hendrick. It was still snowing outside. The bunker had a small woodstove, which was made of heavy gauge sheet metal. The smoke escaped through a pipe, which went out above the doorway. It was forbidden to make fires during clear weather -- day or night -- to prevent the positions from being given away.

The wood snapped and popped, and its heat made it comfortably warm inside the bunker. A petroleum lamp, hanging from the ceiling, emitted a mild light. The five young men sat on a bench and while holding their mess tins on their laps, they spooned-in the soup. "Now this would be the life," Baumann uttered with his bass voice. "It'd be nice -- much too nice," Kolbe replied, and then added, "Eugen and Ole will go to the sauna after we eat and bring back firewood. Franz and Kurt will relief Heinrich and Henry. I will bring Otto and Heinz their food to their emplacement." The door opened suddenly, letting a rush of cold air inside. Untersturmführer Hessler bowed as he entered through the doorway. "Well men, greetings to you!" "Cheerio, Untersturmführer!" This was the way the officers and the men of the Royal Austrian Army had greeted each other during WWI. Kolbe reported that nothing unusual was going on and updated Hessler about the overall situation. Hessler told the men about the heavy fighting going on to the north. The Russians were pushing towards Klin and to the south too. They might be attempting to encircle the spear point of the Army Group Center. Baumann asked if replacements were to be expected. It seemed unlikely that the company would be getting replacements, the company commander said, but the regiment would receive an infantry battalion from the army as reinforcement. The Untersturmführer speculated on the possibility that the division might be pulled out from the front lines to be deployed somewhere in the rear and be replenished.

Going through heavy snowfall, Kolbe brought food to Schmidt and Meyer. The two MG crewmen were almost snowed-in inside their emplacement. They had covered the MG with a shelter-half, and their own selves with another. Visibility was a mere twenty meters. Only their teary eyes looked out from the frost covered hoods. "Nothing's up – shit weather! Eyes burn and cold feet!" It was not a proper military report, but it was an accurate description of what the situation was like. "Take cover under the shelter-half and eat. I'll keep watch so long!" Kolbe said. One should have snow goggles, he thought. That should be possible. He would make the suggestion to the commander coming soon. The Soviet High Command had brought-up seventeen and a half armies by the beginning of December to attack the weakened German Army Group Center. Three of those armies came out of Siberia. Others came out of the Asian parts of the Soviet Union. Some of these had grown to three times or even four times their strength after being replenished with reserves. The Army Group Center was facing an overwhelming foe. It had not received a single fresh division during December. By contrast, the Russian western front was reinforced by thirty three division and thirty nine brigades. These numbers expressed the huge military superiority of men and material the Soviets possessed. Just before dusk, during the 8th of December, an enemy recon team on skis had advanced to just before the company's positions. Baumann and Johannsen had spotted them in time and took them under fire with their machine gun.

Afterwards, they took weapons, ammunition, ham, felt boots and fur caps from the fallen enemy soldiers. A special booty presented the Siberian riflemen's ski equipment. Most of the Landsers were very familiar with the boards, as they called the skis, since childhood. They all stemmed from the mountains. Some came from the Alps, others from the Bohemian Forest, the Erz Mountains, or the Riesengebirge. A wounded man from Irkutskaya was brought to the aid station. He said that his commissar had shot an old woman and a wounded Russian female soldier in Lenino, because they had been "infested" by the fascists. The snowfall stopped the following morning. The enemy's artillery showed its presence. It shot especially at prominent features in the countryside. It was obvious that the Russians were not yet familiar where the German lines meander. Only after the weather had cleared-up did a few Ratas (I-16 fighters) show up and circled above the German positions like hungry vultures. The Germans had already put-out the fires during the first signs of clear weather. That was their luck, because their bunkers would have been targets of the plane's weapons. The machine gun positions too, were covered with white sheets. The sauna hut in the forest, however, had been spotted and was duly shot to flames. A few soldiers were killed there, amongst them Heinrich Hofer and Franz Mikosch. Both losses weighed heavily for the company, but especially for their comrades in Kolbe's squad.

Kolbe wrangled with God and the world. "If they only went to the sauna last night ... why ...?" Why? Eugen Baumann ripped the bunker's door open and shouted, "Because of this damned shitty war ... and the Almighty above only watches ...!" Kolbe packed him by the collar and pulled him into the bunker. "You're not to scream around here. Remember that!" he hissed angrily at Baumann. Baumann sat down on the bench, placed his elbows upon his knees, his head in his hands, and then began to sob. "We're all going crazy ... I think I already am ..." "Only schnapps will help now," Henry Hendrick said, and then he pulled out the bottle of Genever from his coat pocket. "Here, take a drink, then you will all feel better." Immediately thereafter, the enemy's artillery began to fire. With horrid howls, the rockets of the Stalin organs hissed towards their positions and detonated with thunderous flashes. Clouds of snow floated in the air and icy dirt clods were thrown around. It sounded as if all hell broke loose, with a clamor of howling, whistling, and rumbling. Close to the bunkers of Kolbe's squad too, a few projectiles crashed down, and some landed so close that the logs in the ceilings rattled. Kolbe, Baumann and Hendrick were inside the bunker. All three bit their teeth together and ducked with every detonation as if someone hit them on the back of their necks. Then the barrage wandered further to the rear, to inside the forest. "Get out!" Kolbe yelled with a hoarse voice. Hendrick jumped into a foxhole that was nearby Grossert's MG, who had taken it over from Hofer and Meyer.

Baumann ran to the right, over to his first machine gunner Otto Schmidt. Kolbe went into his foxhole, which was situated between both MG emplacements. Sitting on tanks, the enemy advanced quickly in battalion strength. The tracks ground their way into the snow, throwing white dusty clouds behind the tanks. The T-34s took the lead, while the T-26s brought up the rear. Three Sturmgeschütze, four Pak, and an 88 fired out of the woods. The most dangerous weapon for the tanks was the 88. Its anti-tank round could destroy any tank. In short order, the first T-34 stood in the snow like a burning torch, and shortly after that the next tank got hit. The eighty-eight now fired at the T-26s. First, three got hit, and then a fourth. The accompanying infantrymen lie in the snow and fired at the forest's edge, two hundred and fifty meters away. The company still had no permission to fire. Now the enemy tanks had stopped and fired what they could towards the forest. The enemy officers and commissars forced their infantrymen to advance with much shouting and yelling. "Dawai – pashol!" When they had reached a distance of one hundred meters from the German lines, the German infantry opened fire with a sudden fusillade. The effects were terrible. The attackers dropped as if they were mowed down, coloring the snow crimson. The Landsers shot like mad. Loaded and changed barrels as if in a trance. A few enemy soldiers and tanks were already going back. One T-26 went and hid behind a huge straw pile, which stood about one hundred and fifty meters from the German lines. Currently it seemed as if the rest of the enemy tanks had had enough.

The crewmen now knew who they were up against. The infantrymen seemed to know this too, because they also retreated. Many of them were caught in the German gun-fire as they ran. Two more tanks got hit and then stood like burning monuments amongst the dead comrades in the battle field. Ole Johannsen didn't let the tank that went behind the straw out of his sight, so the T-26 should still be behind the snowed-in mound. He would've noticed it if he had changed his position. Why doesn't he get out of there? Johannsen called out to Otto Schmidt, "Behind the pile of hay is still a tank. We could get at it and bust it!" Even before Schmidt could answer, the enemy's artillery began firing again, supported by Stalin organs. Now the enemy knew where the German lines were. The rounds landed damned close to the bunkers and MG positions. A bunker of a neighboring squad over to their right had received a direct hit. Logs and dirt clods were thrown into the air; luckily no comrades were inside it. Grossert's machine gun position was almost hit. Barely five meters behind their location a shell thudded into the solidly frozen ground with a thunderous blast that made the ground quake and inundated the two men with icy chunks. Stinking, acidic powder gasses spread out from there. Meyer shouted angrily, "Dammit ... my head ... where's my helmet?" He had worn his steel helmet only loosely over the fur hat and a frozen dirt clod had knocked it from his head. "My back!" Grossert groaned; he too had got hit by a piece.

Kolbe also had luck, when a shell detonated close to his foxhole and showered him with frozen hunks and a fine mist of snow. The attack rolled again with the tanks in the lead. The Red Army troops hopped like mad through the snow, tripped over their long coats, fell down, fought their way back onto their feet, and shouted with their hoarse and guttural voices, "Uraaah ... uraaah ...!" And once more it was the eighty-eight that was the first to thunder. The sound reverberated through the forest; the first T-34 had stopped with a jolt and then it blew apart with flames and a thunderclap. Meyer shouted, "Encore!" It came straight away. The next tank turned around on its own axis after it had received a hit from the Flak, and then it stopped and smoldered. The enemy was close enough now. "Fire!" The built-up tension was over. Now the German small arms spewed death and destruction against the enemy and forced them to go down. The tanks too had suffered serious losses. They pulled back again and the infantry followed. First, only a few soldiers did so, then whole groups of men ran back. A few dropped into the snow and stayed there lying motionless. The attacker's hoarse shouting had died down and was followed by the moaning of the badly wounded soldiers. The Germans could not help them and their own comrades were not allowed to. It would be dark soon. The alert Swede discovered something that would be very important to the company; on top of the pile of hay the snow had been disturbed.

Ole Johannsen shouted, "Unterscharführer, come over here -- I've discovered something!" "Me too," Kolbe shouted back. "At the haystack -- there's an observer! Run over to the Sturmgeschütz, have them fire high-explosive rounds into it!" Johannsen sprinted like a chased rabbit to the rear and disappeared into the forest. It hadn't taken long before the first shot run out of the woods. With a flash and a boom the shell had exploded on the top of the haystack. Shot after shot followed. Along with the flashes and the straw and snow flying through the air, human body parts could be observed soaring. Alerted by the assault gun's cannonade, the Flak gun and a 37mm Pak joined in on the shooting. A few figures had attempted to flee. However, they did not make it far, because machine gun fire cut them down. The tank's crew had decided it had become too dangerous. The tank attempted to get away when it was fired upon by the Flak gun. It got stopped and burned like a torch near the haystack. Darkness came and spread its veil over the gruesome scenery. The night going from the 9th to the 10th of December had been quiet. Kolbe, Baumann, and Meyer were sitting inside the bunker, and were gathered around the stove in which resinous pine was crackling. Baumann stared over to Kolbe with glassy eyes. "I'm sorry, that ..." Whenever he's touched, he uses the dialect of his mountainous homeland, Kärnten. Kolbe padded his shoulder in a comradely way. "It's all right." He reached a cigarette over to Baumann. "Peace pipe ..." "In two weeks it'll be Christmas,"

Meyer said silently and swallowed hard. "If we're still alive until then?" "Now let's not get sentimental, Heinz. We'll make it somehow," Kolbe said and took a deep drag. After the quiet night, it seemed that the 10th of December could be a day without hard fighting. Along the lines of the two battalions belonging to the Regiment DF a light artillery harassment fire went down. Kolbe and Johannsen were sleeping inside their bunker. Both had made an excursion out into the fore field during the previous night and had retrieved some submachine gun ammunition. Thereby a lightly wounded enemy soldier had been encountered, over by the haystack, who was attempting to sleep through his vodka induced drunkenness. If they had not found him and awakened him, he may have very well frozen to death. He had been brought to the rear to be interrogated. What would he think after he was sober again? Three Ratas showed-up again during noontime. They were suddenly there. In low altitude they floated over the lines. The red stars could be clearly seen on the bottom of their wings. The Landsers quickly pulled the white sheets over their heads and ducked down low. At once, the planes went into a dive and with thundering engines they flew over the positions. The men could feel the gush of cold air going over their heads. Grossert lifted his sheet a little and looked into the pale blue sky. "They're coming back," he bellowed. The three fighters were approaching the company's sector again, coming in low. Their on- board weapons shot out flames and burped. Grossert yelled frantically, "Heinz, now it's our turn!"

Then the Soviet fighters thundered overhead. A metallic noise sounded out. Grossert's MG got hit and was thrown a bit away. The projectile ricocheted into the forest. The incoming rounds thudded into the ground and went past the foxholes. Round after round, and one could see the deadly tracks in the snow. "That was a close one," Heinz Meyer said in relief. The Ratas didn't return, because two Me- 109s had suddenly appeared. Grossert crawled over to his MG. "Kiss my ass!" he called out to Meyer. "The butt is destroyed and so are the receiver and the return spring. Over and out! It's ruined!" Grossert collected the pieces. Gruffly, he told Meyer, "Heinz, I'm going to bring the wreckage into the bunker and grab a Russian MG. I'll be back shortly and …" He went away and came back unscathed, because both friend and foe were distracted by the air-to air fighting, which was going on in the clear blue skies towards Ivanovskoje. The Ratas had no chance against the Me-109s, despite their superior numbers. Two Russian fighters went down in flames. The third fighter attempted to flee, but was caught and also went down, burning. Shortly afterwards, both German fighters flew over the lines and wiggled with their wing tips, made a turn, and then went to attack the Russian artillery and rocket launcher positions. The Soviet Flak fired like crazy, but missed, and also ended-up as victims to the fighters. The Men's moods had improved lately. They had regained new confidence, which was curbed again come evening, when orders were given out for another retreat!

"We've been here only a few days," Grossert said to Kolbe. "What is going on here?" "It is called shortening of the front lines," the Unterscharführer said grimly. "I wouldn't be surprised if we are to be the rear guards again," Grossert grumbled. He didn't have to wonder because their company did get chosen to cover the retreat. They were to go back just before mid-night. The new defensive lines were behind the Istra River. Pioniers had built useful positions there. It was not far – about twelve kilometers. "This time we'll have it easier," Kolbe said. "We have the captured Siberian skis." Ole Johannsen crinkled his forehead. "It's still no pleasure, going at night through the woods." After dusk, both battalions pulled back, leaving two companies behind. The enemy remained quiet. Only occasionally would a flare shoot up into the darkness, or a shot be fired, probably from a nervous sentry. The skiers of the company went to patrol the positions in pairs. One had to be watchful to the utmost. Since the past evening, clouds had covered the sky again and vision was impaired by the snowfall. The skiers were glad to be able to move about again. Especially the Swede, Ole Johannsen, who was a good crosscountry skier, was glad to be on skis again and glide through the area. Brander's squad, which was completely equipped with skis, would bring up the rear of the rear guard. Weapons at the ready, slung before their chests, ammo boxes slung over their shoulders, and rucksacks upon their backs – this was how they disappeared into the dark forest.

Within it, the snow was deep and loose. The snowing stopped after a little while, the clouds opened-up to allow the moon's pale light to fall upon cleared areas, broken into a thousand shadows by the branches. The forest had acquired a different look. Stripes and spots glowed in fantastic forms between the deep shadows. This frustrated proper vision more so than even an unvarying darkness. The squad had arrived at the forest roadway. Vision was better here, and the snow had been flattened by the traffic. Almost completely soundless they glided along. In the moonlight, the snow sparkled on the huge trees as if a million diamonds were hanging in them. Here, there remained some of primeval creation, there was still wilderness, which dies and gets reborn. The forest looked magically, with the snow cover and the frost. With moss dangling down and covered with frost, the trees appeared like specters of old sagas. Some of the men shuddered in reverence. Otto Schmidt was almost mesmerized by the sight. He even forgot the war for a while. Even Ole Johannsen seemed to be affected. He said quietly, "Like Thule, the symbol of an island of happiness, far to the north." No one said a word now. They all were enthralled by the magic of this harsh, icy world. The new lines were located behind the Istra River, which was covered by thick ice and a deep layer of snow. The defensive emplacements had been laid-out in similar fashion as the previous positions, and were not far from the medium- sized city of Istra, which was located about half a kilometer east of the same named river.

The city could be seen from afar. It was spread far apart on top of a ridge and a small river went half-way around it. On another ridge, branching out from the main one and running east to west, sat the cathedral of Istra. Its towers were visible to quite a distance. Also on top were six church-like buildings, of which the mightiest was a beautiful old church. Deployed to the left of the Division Das Reich was the 5 th Panzer Division, which had arrived just in November. The neighbor to the right was pulled over the river far towards the west. This left the right wing of the Division Das Reich completely open. It was so in similar fashion with the 5 th Panzer Division on their left wing. Brandner's squad had occupied their bunker and positions just before dawn of the 11 th of December. Shortly thereafter, the first firefight with an enemy reconnaissance team had already started over by their left neighbor. So, the enemy was already here! "One can't even take a kitty-nap before the shit starts again!" Hendrick ranted. The company commander entered the bunker. Kolbe stood at attention and wanted to make a proper report. Hessler just waved a hand. He's dog tired too. His face showed signs of the hard times. Groaning, he sat down beside Kolbe by the stove and warmed his cold hands over the hot surface. "I had to write a report and almost froze my fingers off." "When will we get replacements or even relieved?" Unterscharführer Kolbe asked. Hessler raised his shoulders.

"No one knows for certain. Next week or next month – who knows ...?" The veins in Kolbes forehead swelled. His face turned red with anger. He's fighting for words, and then it burst out of him, "Are we the sacrificial lambs here! This is against all military reasoning. Not to mention being inhumane! One doesn't even treat animals this way!" "One doesn't let an animal suffer – you shoot it when it collapsed!" the Untersturmführer said and sank his head tiredly. Kolbe took a hold of his arm. "Hey, old buddy," he said a little startled. "You're not going to break down? Come on, drink some hot tee." Hessler pulled himself together and slurped some tee. "It does really help," he said. Then he got back on his feet with one swing. "Thanks, fellows – I must go on now." When he had left the bunker, Kolbe told Hendrick, "Don't say a word about this to anyone!" Hendrick shook his head. "Not me!" The 11th of December began with an overcast sky; only later would it get lighter. The sun, however, could not shine through the cloud cover. Standing on the gentle slopes east of the river were the deeply snowed-in forests, which seemed to be hiding something. It did not take long for the silent forest to reveal its secrete. Suddenly, the guard posts up front could hear the plop-plop sound of heavy mortars, and then the ugly sound of dropping mortar rounds. Instinctively, they cowered inside their cover and made themselves as small as possible. Then it rumbled and flashed. Fountains of snow, mixed with frozen chunks, got thrown up.

Then a new volley announced itself. The ground quaked and one almost thought to hear it moaning with pain. Then the enemy came forward. With infantry sitting on them, a few tanks went across the frozen surface of the river. "Oh my goodness!" Grossert said with dread. "Masses of Ivans – today they're going to take us by the scruff of the neck!" "Just stay calm, men!" Untersturmführer Hessler called-out. "Aim at the infantry ... let them roll over us ... get the close-combat gear ready!" "I hope our foxhole will withstand the weight!" Heinz Meyer exclaimed. "It'll hold!" The combat engineers had blown the holes deeply into the solidly frozen ground. Now, the enemy assault force was only two hundred meters away. The Sturmgeschütze, painted white and barely visible to the enemy at this distance, began to open fire. Two T-34s had stopped rolling and emitted smoke. Crying out with fright, the enemy troops dropped down from the tanks. Shortly thereafter, the tanks blew into smithereens. Now the enemy had approached to within one hundred meters. "Fire!" The tanks stopped and were firing at the German lines with highexplosive shells. Then with machine guns firing, they came closer. They revved-up their engines occasionally. From within their cover, the Germans fired at the attacking Red Army troops, whose hoarse battle cries got weaker as they approached closer and closer to the German defensive lines. Their ranks were getting thinner. They finally stopped their charge and, lying in the snow, they refused to continue, despite terrible threats from their officers and commissars.

Only a few went on, threatened by the weapons of the own superiors, they followed the tanks. The Germans had no other choice. They had to get out of their cover, otherwise it would be over. over. "Get out and on them!" the company commander cried out, as they were in the tank's blind spots. Shouting out loud, weapons at the hips and firing, they charged the enemy while keeping low. The tanks drove on, throwing snow up and behind them as they rolled. The men got involved in hand-to-hand fighting with a superior force. The surprised Red Army troopers defended themselves bravely against the angrily attacking Landsers. Submachine guns and rifles barked, machine guns fired short bursts, spades were bared, and a grim and horse shouting echoed over the field of combat. Two, three tanks had stopped and turned to grind their tracks over the foxholes and bunkers. The rest continued onward, not paying attention to the own infantry. Then help arrived just in the nick of time! Tanks, which belonged to the 5th Panzer Division, but had been allotted to the Division Das Reich, had arrived. They attacked immediately, and several enemy tanks stood in flames in short order. The rest pulled back in haste. The enemy infantry too, gave up the fight. Kolbe's earthen bunker was slightly damaged, but still usable as shelter. Henry Hendrick was lying inside the bunker; he had a bullet stuck in his shoulder. Heinz Meyer sat beside him with a bandaged head. He had a laceration, which had been caused by a bash from a rifle-butt. The fur cap had buffered the blow somewhat. Now he sat there with a throbbing head.

He most likely would not have had a laceration, had he worn his helmet. "When my headache is a little better, I'll go back outside," he told Hendrick. "How're you doing?" "To say shitty would still not be telling you half! These damned lice, these blood-suckers have made their way through the bandage. I'm going to go crazy!" "Just remember, soon you will be de-loused and lying in white sheets, singing Christmas carols. A pretty young nurse will bring you roast goose and Christmas pastry to your bed." Kolbe peered inside. "How're you doing? Good? Fine then. The company suffered five dead and six wounded. Now we're only twenty two men left ..." "You can strike me from the wounded list, I'm staying here!" said Heinz Meyer. Kolbe's bearded and shrunken face showed a thin smile. "That's what I thought. I hope you won't regret it." Kolbe hadn't been gone long, when the enemy's artillery began a cannonade with all sizes of guns including Stalin organs. As the shells started to wander to the rear, Heinz Meyer got ready. "Well then, Henry. You'll be brought to the HVP11) when it's dark out. If we shall not see each other again, I'll wish you well now. Make it good through the winter." "You too, Heinz, and greet the comrades for me." The next attack had also been beaten back with much blood, despite the enemy's superiority in numbers. The weather got milder. It was only a few degrees below freezing. The Landsers breathed a sigh of relief. This was how it could stay until Christmas, and then it could get even nicer, they thought.

Warm food came to the emplacements during the night, and it even stayed warm in the food containers. They also received mail. Whoever didn't have guard duty, sat beside a petroleum lamp in the bunkers and read the words from home. Untersturmführer Hessler sat in his bunker and wrote down the losses for the first sergeant, Stabscharführer Lauterbach. Hessler sighed, "It's looking bad, Lauterbach. The generals standing at the green tables are probably calculating with full-strength divisions and battalions ..." The first sergeant lowered his head. "It is too bad for all the young and hopeful men. Their youthful adulthood had barely got started and then it's already over." The nightly sky was covered with only a diffuse layer of clouds. Here and there a flare wiggled up and then came back down with pale light. Sometimes a shot rang out or a short MG garb fired into the fore field. Then it was silent once more. What the men didn't known yet on this 11 th of December was that this European war had grown into a world war. On this day, Adolf Hitler had spoken in the Reichstag to make known that, among other things, due to the Anti- Comintern Pact, he had issued passports to the American ambassador. On that same day, foreign minister von Ribbentrop announced to the American ambassador that, as of now, Germany was at war with the US. At the same time, Mussolini proclaimed the same for Italy. At dawn, during December the 12th, while a peaceful fog billowed over the river, the enemy's artillery obliterated the stillness.

Since it was only just below freezing, the men had jumped into their foxholes and trenches just before the barrage. Kolbe's squad now had only six men and the MG crew. The men got startled as a heavy mortar round slammed into their bunker. Snow and debris of boards and logs were thrown into the air. A few of the pieces landed in the snow near Ole Johannsen. "Shit! Food, ammunition and mess kits are all ruined!" he shouted angrily. He then realized that he or other comrades would've paid with their lives, had they been inside there. The fighting started again – the enemy attacked. The Siberians hung onto the tanks as they emerged from the dark fog. The German tanks and Sturmgeschütze opened fire immediately. Soon, several of the T-34s stood still, burning like torches. Death had reaped a rich crop amongst the Red Army troops. The air was filled with shots from every type of weapon. The Sturmgeschütze now left the enemy tanks to the own Panzer to deal with. They fired high- explosive shells directly into the attacking ranks of the enemy. The attack had begun to falter. It was carried out only haphazardly now, until it came to a full standstill. The enemy was pulling back once more. Soviet ground attack planes arrived in the afternoon, yet caused little damage, because the German dual 20mm Flak guns fired like crazy. One plane had received a direct hit, and its pieces crashed down behind the German defensive positions. Since Kolbe's squad didn't have a bunker anymore, they were allowed to be quartered inside the company command post.

At night, there were only two or three of the six-man squad inside the bunker anyhow. Kolbe, Kirchner, and Grossert had gone out into the fore field to retrieve mess kits, ammunition, and food from the dead Siberian soldiers. Nothing happened, except that a few flares were fired. The sky was overcast and not a star could be spotted. It was still. Once in a while, only some rumbling could be heard far to the north and the south-west. It seemed as if something was brewing together there. It took only three quarters of an hour for the three "body strippers", as the company messenger, Andreas Anholzer, called them, to return with rich pickings. Now everyone had a mess kit again, which first had to be thoroughly cleaned, though. On the 13th of December, the Soviets peppered the German

lines with sporadic artillery fire. There were, however, no attacks. The muffled sound of combat to
the north and southwest, had wandered ever more
towards the west. The Landsers came to the con-
clusion that the enemy must've broken through to
the left of the 5 th Panzer Division and to the
right of their own division. And this assumption
was correct. Slowly, but surly, the ring tightened
ever more. The Regiment DF was surrounded for
the first time! Only yesterday, had Untersturmführer Hessler mulled over another time, when the
30,000 Bavarian troops, which had marched into
Russia as a contingent of Naploeon's army, took
and went into Moscow, got decimated, and then
went under. Only a small, bedraggled and sick
number of them had made it back home.

May the Almighty beware us of this fate! It had
become illusionary to hold on to the Istra lines any
longer. They reckoned with a retreat soon, since a
German counterattack was out of the question. The
decision had been made on the 15 th of December.
Another retreat westward was ordered and pulled-
through. In the meantime, the cold had returned
full force and more snow had started to fall. The
Regiment DF had been designated as the rear guard
once again. The division pulled back at midnight.
Due to continued snowfall and snowdrifts, the roads
were in an unbelievably bad condition. A large
portion of the vehicles got hopelessly stuck and had
to be destroyed. To be separated from their vehicles, which they had used for so long, was visibly
a tough thing for the men. Hessler's company, which

had a total combat strength of twenty two men, was the last unit to pull out of the lines after midnight. Kolbe, Grossert, and Meyer brought-up the rear. They did not have the skis anymore, since they had been destroyed by the direct hit into their bunker. Now they had to wade through the snow, which was knee deep at times. The wind drove icy cold from the northeast, blowing over the deeply snowed-in countryside. Grossert heard skiers approaching, despite the noise of the wind, because he kept on lifting the earflaps of his cap and turned to listen towards his rear. Quickly, he reported it. Kolbe told Grossert and Meyer to take-up positions on both sides of the road. He stayed on the path and while he knelt down, he cocked his submachine gun.

Only a few minutes later, the first shadows emerged from the snowfall. They were at most eight or ten meters away. Kolbe pulled the trigger; barely a second later both Grossert and Meyer did the same. Their shots mixed with the howling northeasterner, and their bullets mowed the first few Siberians down. The rest took cover and returned fire. Kolbe noticed that the enemy wanted to surround them. He called out to his comrades; "Go – get out of here. I'll cover you! Go twenty meters and then you give me cover …" Grossert and Meyer disappeared into the darkness and snowfall. The Red Army troopers, who had of course heard his voice, fired at him with their MPs. A few rounds whistled razor sharp past his ears. "Dammit!" he grumbled grimly through clenched teeth. Grossert and Meyer had taken-up positions and let their MPs bark. They aimed at the small muzzle flashes from the enemy's weapons, which were distracted by Kolbe. Kolbe sprang up and ran stooped-over following the tracks in the snow. "I'm coming!" he shouted. As they were about to go on, their MG crew arrived. Otto Schmidt asked out of breath if everyone is all right. They were. "I'll show them!" Kolbe said. "Otto and Eugen stay on the road with the MG. Kurt and Ole spread out to the left, and Heinz goes with me to the right. We're going to stay quiet and let them approach. When I fire the first shot, you all fire too. Got it?" Full of concentration, they stared and listened into the dark-grey snow shower.

The Swede heard a scraping type of noise, then how someone cursed under his breath as he fell down. That was really close by. All of a sudden, Grossert saw a large shadow before him. Instinctively, he pulled the trigger. He could no longer have waited for Kolbe's initiating fire. Ole Johannsen followed suit. The enemy had not fired back. They could only hear a heavy wheezing, which, all of a sudden, stopped a short time later. The other comrades had remained quiet. The enemy did too, for the time being. After a while, a voice came over from the path called two names, but no one answered. The Siberian called out the names once more, and then he left the path. As Kurt and Ole saw a hazy shadow, they fired at it. The figure dropped to the ground without making a sound. It remained eerily quiet, and even the wind had died down. The snowfall had increased, however. What now? The senses were strained and the cold was penetrating the clothes. Kolbe had decided what to do. "We'll take off the skis from the fallen enemy. The Russians are certainly all dead." "Kurt, Ole," he called out – and just then a submachine gun blasted at him! Grossert and Johannsen fired back immediately. After one of the Siberians had shouted, "Sjuda! Germanski okokaj! (Come on, German, drop dead)" Kolbe shouted back, "You can have it yourself! Kurt, Ole, go!" Staying low, they sprang forward, fired their weapons from the hips, and tripped over figures lying in the snow. They halted when they noticed that there was no one fighting back.

"Put the skis on and then let's get away from here!" Kolbe said, panting. From all their former pursuers, no one had remained alive. They had been lucky again, but for how much longer? Everyone had boards on their feet once again. Breathing heavily, they skimmed through the darkness and snowfall. When dawn had approached, they approached one of the lookouts from their battalion, placed at the edge of a forest. Soon, they were back in their unit, where they were happily greeted. "It's great to have you back. I had just been making preparations to go with Kirchner and Anholzer to search for you," Hessler said relieved. After Kolbe had made a brief report, the company commander assigned them to take up positions in a glade inside the forest to secure the right wing. Soon thereafter, the Siberians had arrived in front of the German defensive lines, gliding on skis. Here they came upon an enemy that was admittedly inferior in numbers, but who was just as familiar with forests as they were. After enemy reconnaissance teams had sought a gap in the lines, but were repulsed each time, they attempted their luck over at the right wing, by Brandner's squad. It was snowing only lightly now. Ole Johannsen's breath was taken away when he looked across the glade. He saw men moving through the trees, wearing white camouflage uniforms. On the right edge of the glade, a few figures were approaching directly towards Schmidt's MG position. Kolbe, Schmidt, and the rest of the comrades too, were watching the assault detachment, which was advancing from tree to tree.

When the Siberians had approached to within thirty meters, Kolbe opened fire at the enemy group closest to him. Schmidt's MG commenced firing right after Kolbe's initiating bursts. One garb after another swept over the cleared area. Many Red Army troopers dropped into the snow. A few fled in panic, but were hampered by the deep snow and scrub, and were then cut down by the torrent of bullets. Others yet, were firing back blindly. However, the Germans were hard to spot. A number of enemy soldiers had burrowed themselves into the snow and fired back, but then fountains of snow sprung up all around them and their fire ceased. In time, the Siberian had established the lay of the German positions. Their bullets whipped into the trees, behind which the Germans were firing from.

Schmidt heard a threatening ricochet. At the same time he heard an unidentifiable sound beside him. He glanced over, and cried out when he saw his buddy, Eugen. Baumann's fur hat sat crookedly upon his head. His head hung loosely on top of the submachine gun receiver and blood trickled into the snow from his head. Frightened, Otto Schmidt shook Baumann's arm. "Hey, Eugen ...!" A painful moan was the answer. Then Baumann turned his head, showing a blood covered face. "Otto ... I think the Siberians have scalped me ..." "The scalp is still there. But they gave you a new parting in your hair. Give me your bandage pack!" "Watch out! It was the one behind that thick tree over there. I'm going to burn one into him." "You're doing nothing.

Stay down, so I can wrap you up better!" The snow crunched behind the two men. It was Unter-sturmführer Hessler and the driver, Philipp Leitner, called Fips the whistler. "Is it bad?" asked Hessler. "I'm feeling a bit weird," Baumann answered. "You're coming with me," the company commander said to Baumann. "Leitner will stay here instead. He doesn't have a vehicle anymore anyways." Another good comrade less, Otto Schmidt thought. "Take it easy, Eugen ..." Baumann wobbled away alongside the commander. "I will, I will, Otto," he brought out sadly. The bush warfare continued until nightfall. It had been carried out with much hos-tility on both sides. Finally, the enemy went back. The next retreat was during the night of 17th December. And this was how it went day after day, night after night. Through Sloboda, Kiskovo,

Kurova, Schervinsky, all the way to behind the Rusa River by Borovina. It was a hard march for the half-starved and tired soldiers in the field-gray uniforms. They had to fend off attacks by superior enemy forces by day, and during the night, they had to bite their teeth together and march through knee-deep snow in icy cold temperatures -- thirty to forty kilometers. Always going further back ... The last leg of the journey was taken during the night of the 20th December. In an ice-cold snow-storm, which caused deep drifts, the hard march continued towards Borovino, which lies by the Rusa River. They put one foot before the other like robots and stemmed their bodies against the on-slaught of the icy storm that attacked them like a wild animal.

The cold went through the clothes and almost al-lowed the blood to freeze in the veins. The barbaric cold bit the hooded faces, where only the eyes peered out. Don't get weak now, the Landsers talked into their own selves over and over, even though they would have gladly thrown away their back-packs or MG ammunition boxes, because the stuff was gradually getting too heavy. The MG slings were digging painfully into their shoulders. The storm, which was blowing the snow in dense masses, was getting stronger, and the cold got worse -- down to fifty degrees below zero centigrade. Some were so exhausted that they dropped into the snow and wanted to freeze to death so that the inhumane torture would finally end. The burden the soldiers had to tolerate increased. The men had to perform far more than they could endure. "Thank the Almighty!" Untersturmführer Hessler groaned, as they arrived at the Rusa River in the dawn of the 21 st of December. The exhausted men were a pitiful sight, with their grimy snow shirts. The Führer should see us now, Hessler thought. A few of his other fellow sufferers were thinking the same thing. The Soviets attacked with strong forces even as the regimental commander, Obersturmbannführer (Lieutenant Colonel) Kumm, discussed with his two battalion commanders over the placement of forward posts in the reconnoitered areas. They forewent on having forward posts under these circumstances. The Regiment DF took-up positions on the west bank of the Rusa and readied for defense.

They had a line to defend that was six kilometers long, and only five or six big holes had been dug to provide cover. Even as the battalions were being marshaled to the positions, the enemy attacked with superior forces. Before long, strong forces, with the support of tanks, had broken through by the 3rd Battalion. "Get back into the holes!" the battalion commander shouted. "Give each other covering fire!" Gunfire from MGs, MPs, and rifles sang out like taught wires. Moaning, the exhausted Landsers tripped and hobbled back. Many didn't even take cover. They knew that once they lie down they won't be able to get back up. A few did take cover and fired at the oncoming enemy, and helped their other comrades to regain their courage. With grim anger the Germans went against the enemy. Over here, they got to the tank's blind side, and over there they were visible again. They gave more than they could, and cursed God and the whole world. Their breath came out as steam and froze into a thick ice crust on the mouth pieces of their hoods "Oh, mother!" Heinz Meyer called out. "I can't go on anymore!" "Forward!" the commander shouted. "This means pure survival now!" The young men pulled themselves together and wobbled onward. They must push back the enemy, to finally end this gruesomeness. With grim anger, the overtired Landsers stormed forward and threw back the enemy in hand-to- hand fighting with high losses. It was an unbelievable scene. Afterwards, the totally exhausted men simply let themselves drop into the snow.

The eighty-eight guns, standing further in the rear, had stopped the enemy tanks that had broken through. A few of them were destroyed, while the rest retreated. "Get up!" the company commander shouted to his men, who were lying in the snow. "Tanks are approaching from the rear! Do you want to be crushed?" Groaning, they rose. Two T-26s came swaying back and forth and without accompanying infantry. Quickly, the men made bundle charges out of stick-grenades. The last tank had to be taken first. Kolbe wanted to do this. The engine noise was getting closer, they would soon be here. Kolbe carefully lifted his head. Twenty meters, fifteen – now the second tank was even up with him, at a distance of five to six meters. Kolbe rose and pulled the fuse-cord as he ran, and then he threw the charge under the turret. He ran away as fast as he still could and threw himself amongst some dead Russians. A very loud bang sounded out, and the T-26 came to a dead stop a few meters further on and smoking. As the tankists opened a hatch to get out, a huge boom followed. Flames shot out of the hatches and the tank blew apart by the force of the detonations of its own ammunition. The pressure wave almost knocked the lead tank over; it came to a stop. The tank commander opened his hatch and looked surprised over to his burning companion; then he disappeared lightning quick and wanted to close the hatch again. At this moment, stick and egg hand grenades came flying towards the turret, of which two or three found their way inside to explode immediately afterwards.

This tank too, stood in the battlefield as a burning monument of a gruesome war, surrounded by the dead. It had quieted down. After the Landsers had unthawed bread and bacon on top of the hot armor plates of the destroyed tanks and eaten, they commenced to dig their foxholes. Together with the combat engineers, they broke up the frozen ground with bore-charges and Teller mines. They did it despite all signs indicating the impossibility of holding these lines throughout the winter. After three days of unbelievably hard work, interrupted repeatedly by attacks of superior enemy forces, the positions by the Rusa were ready. During these times of greatest crisis, many military leaders believed that only a general withdrawal of forces, back into properly build defensive lines, could prevent the entire front from collapsing. Hitler, however, used all his willpower to go against these wishes. He categorically forbade all retreat. Serious disputes with the German Chief of Staff of the army ensued, over issues like combat leadership, the supply situation, and organization. Field Marshal von Brauchitsch could no longer stand-up to the increased burdens. He asked to be relieved, and was dismissed from service on December the 19th 1941. Adolf Hitler himself took over as commander in chief of the army during these hardest of hours, since he was deeply convinced that his persona and the providence behind his orders, alone, would give the faltering army the necessary drive for a breakthrough. The troops seemed to have gained new impetus through his decision in December 1941.

His uncompromising way of implementing his order, whereby all voluntary withdrawals were forbidden, led to many small crises, but in the end prevented a larger catastrophe, and the attacking strength of the Soviet armies were consumed by the stubborn resistance of the German troops. Of course, there was bitter resistance by the military leaders due to Hitler's accustomed manner of contradicting his decisions. This resulted in a constant change of top military leaders, which also brought with it changes of leaders on the front lines themselves. Even Guderian, the father of modern armored warfare, and Hoeppner, two of many, had been struck by Hitler's ban, as they took certain situations in their own hands when it had been deemed necessary to do so, and ordered retreats, or refused to follow orders. Hitler had been proven right during this crisis, however. The tactic to hold the cohesive lines, and to defend important junctions and supply centers any which way that could, was successful. However, it caused the troops and material to be worn-out. General Jodl wrote over Hitler's way of commanding during those times: I had never admired Hitler more than during the winter of 1941 to 1942, were he alone had brought the wavering eastern front to come to a halt, were his willpower and determination had trickled to the frontlines itself, exactly as it had occurred during the last war, when Hindenburg and Ludendorf had stepped forward to take over leadership of the army. Any other illustration is wrong and is a slap in the face of historic truth...

The news that Hitler had taken-over supreme command of the army was a bombshell to the young soldiers of the Regiment Der Führer. This had made their hearts beat faster. They regained their courage and confidence, since them too, the Waffen-SS, belonged to the army. "Now he must break with old traditions and refuse compromises, as he did in 1934, when he chose the Reichswehr (German army during the Weimar Republic) over Roehm. Get rid of the old boy's club, which had sent us into a winter war without being properly equipped," Untersturmführer Paul Hessler told Unterscharführer Helmut Kolbe with excitement. Kolbe too had received this news with positive feelings. He said, "Yes – away with the old stogies and wannabe strategists, who would still rather attack with drums, fife, and waving flags." The Landsers were sitting around in their bunkers, MG positions, and foxholes again, just like back at the Istra lines. The single emplacements were spread far apart, oft times up to one hundred meters. A back-up trench-line or reserves were not available. Those of which that were off duty and were able to warm-up an hour or two could count themselves lucky, because it was icy cold outside. The snowstorms were especially feared, because they could cover up a guard post, cowering in his foxhole with snow. Due to the deep snow drifts, the traffic to and from the front lines could be upheld only through so- called panje sleds. These were often disturbed by the enemy's artillery fire, which caused losses to important supply items. Two days now, was Xaver Unterburger back to the unit.

He had been wounded in September. Now he was back as a real winter warrior, equipped with brand new winter clothing; fur- lined anorak, pants and felt boots! The men marveled at him. "All dolled-up." Kurt Grossert said. "Let's not be jealous," Unterburger replied. "Everyone here will surly get these types of clothing too." The enemy artillery suddenly fired with incredible force during the morning hours of the 23rd of December. With ear-shattering noise the shells and rockets came down over the thinly manned German lines and detonated in the rock hard frozen, snow covered ground. The explosions grew out of the surface as if by conjuring. Smoke inundated the air. Wherever the shells slammed in they had left big dark holes in the snow. A shower of snow dust and icy chunks came down. Salve after salve came over the German positions. "Soon it'll start again," Grossert bellowed to Heinz Meyer. They both cowered in the bottom of their foxhole along with their new MG-34, which they had received only two days ago. Meyer pointed towards the enemy. "There they are! This time without tanks." Now the few guns of the own artillery batteries, infantry howitzers and Sturmgeschütze, tried to create something that resembled a curtain of fire before the own lines. The impacts didn't stop the enemy. Even though a few fell, the masses continued to charge … My God! Xaver Unterburger thought. Who should stop these masses? This type of experience had been cause for nightmares during his convalescence. Now it was real again.

At this moment the enemy had approached to within one hundred meters before the German lines. Their guttural "Uraah" shouting got louder – their outlines bigger. Out of fear to what would happen next, they bunched together and thus made themselves a worthwhile target. "Fire!" the company commander shouted as loudly as he could. Each and every infantry weapon began to fire at once. One Sturmgeschütz and one forward standing field-gun fired right into the attacking masses with high-explosive shells and caused heavy losses. The enemy troops jumped over their dead comrades, who had attacked for nothing. The first volley had already caused many of the attackers to panic. They went to go back to the rear, but their commissars and officers drove them back to the front. Those of which that hadn't been wounded or killed took cover behind the bodies of their dead comrades. The Landsers spotted the commissars and officers and took aim at them. Now, the Red Army troops couldn't be held back anymore. They hastened to go back, and no one stopped them. Only the German machine gun reaped a rich crop amongst their files. The Russians must have recognized the fact that victory could not be achieved during this phase of the fighting. They ceased to carry-on the massive attacks, and only their artillery remained active, firing mostly harassment fire and especially further to the rear in the supply routes. Yet despite this the supplies managed to get through during the night of the 24th of December.

Besides receiving food, ammunition, cigarettes and liquor, the men also finally got proper winter clothing issued. It was the same type of clothing that Xaver Unterburger had on; fur-lined anoraks, pants, felt boots, fur coats, and white camouflage shirts. Together with all this, the men got fresh, warm underwear and socks. Some of the men had tears of joy... finally! Had they received these clothes weeks ago, many a comrade would still be amongst them. In the middle of the issuing process, the regimental commander, Otto Kumm, appeared. He shook hands with his men and spoke words to help raise their spirits. He didn't get to meet many of the men, because they were on watch inside the ice cold foxholes. The commander was impressed by his men's optimism and determination. "And what do you say about the high visit?" Kolbe asked

Schmidt and Grossert. "Snappy, just as the Prussians usually are," Grossert said. Schmidt nodded. "Right, he is polished, Kumm ... nice of him to come the Kumm ..." Unterscharführer Kolbe grinned. Despite Greater Germany, they are and always will be Austrians. Soon thereafter, they went to the front to relief Johannsen and Meyer. Kolbe went to the company command post. There he drank with his friend Hessler a strong swallow of Steinhäger, and after they wished each other a merry Christmas, they tromped out into the still, clear night, going from guard post to guard post to wish a restful and merry Christmas. The enemy remained quiet, as if they didn't want to ruin the holiest of events.

Only sometimes did a flare or a single shot from somewhere remind them that a war was going on in the world. "Back home they're going to services right about now," Hessler said in a low tone. The church would be filled with incense and the dampness of people's breath, which walk in a single file over the cold stone floor to their seats. And then they would become meditative, the old and young, listening to the ancient song; They Were Sheppard to Bethlehem. The first day of Christmas had brought another surprise. At noontime a few Ju-52 cargo planes appeared and dropped-off additional supplies. A westerly wind blew part of the containers, hanging on parachutes, over to the Red Army troops, however. The Landsers cursed. "We shot flares into the air -- they should've been able to see where we are and in which direction the wind is blowing!" The company got to keep one container, even though they had retrieved two. Everything was shared in a comradely manner, no one would be short-changed. This was an unwritten law. Everyone was satisfied with the way everything was distributed; only Xaver Unterburger still ranted over the aircrews that had dropped the good stuff over at the other field post office number 12). The constant tirade got on Kolbe's nerves. "Haven't you understood yet that they did that on purpose to show them boneheads over there how good we have it? That's what one calls higher tactics!" Xaver's eyes widened. "Ohh, that's how it is – got it!"

Besides some harassment fire from the enemy artillery and temperature of minus forty degrees centigrade, the first day of Christmas also brought with it Hitler's order to hold on, belated by almost two weeks, and contentious among the troop leaders. Under personal efforts, supreme commanders, commanders, and officers shall force the troops to fanatical resistance and to keep them in their positions, even as the enemy breaks through the flanks or appears from the rear. Only after reserve forces have manned the rear area defensive sinew positions, will it be allowed to even think about falling back. Since the term sinew position was new to them, they asked their superiors. Unterscharführer Kolbe sent them on to Untersturmführer Hessler. The company commander explained that it may mean something like a bow string, for shooting off arrows. This meant that the troops were to be "flung" out of a sinew position, so-to-speak. The Landsers made their own reason out of this. A "sinew position" is a position you wished for, but would remain a dream. They had their experiences with so-called "winter positions". The enemy remained quiet except for light harassment fire from his artillery on the second day of Christmas. The men didn't contemplate too much about a general order given out by the supreme commander of Army Group Center, Field Marshal Kluge. They just acknowledged it. Each man must hold where he is; he who does not will cause a gap in the line that cannot be filled. Then the following sentence attenuated this order some. Retreat makes only then sense and serves a purpose when it brings about a more favorable condition for fighting, and when possible, to form reserves.

And finally, was followed by a constraint. Each retreat, from division on upwards, needs my personal approval. Light snowfall started again during the night of 27th of December, and the temperatures went up a few degrees. Just before dawn, an enemy combat patrol attempted to take-out Grossert and Meyers's MG nest, but was spotted by Meyer in the nick of time, who took them under fire with his captured MP. The combat team pulled back immediately, leaving two dead behind, lying about fifteen meters before their position. Kolbe and Leitner went ahead and followed the enemy for a short distance, and then they halted and fired a few garbs after them with their submachine guns. The two men took the rucksacks away from the dead Siberians. Their pockets were searched for any papers, and their weapons and reserve magazines — the most important booty — were also taken. The rucksacks contained the usual items like smoked bacon, bread, machorka tobacco, newspapers, and packages of ammunition. "I'll roast you guys some bacon in a moment," Kolbe told Grossert and Meyer. "Leitner will bring it to you when he comes to relieve you." The day was quiet. Each strong point had one sentry out. More ammunition and food in insulated containers came to the lines in the evening. Cold rations were also distributed. Only the eagerly awaited mail didn't come. The first sergeant, however, had brought the men some newspapers, which were fervently read, despite them being two or three weeks old.

Therein, it told of Hitler's refusal to make use of a Russian voluntary army, which wanted to fight side-by- side with the Germans to help free their country of Bolshevism. Most of the Landsers were disappointed by Hitler's decision. The Swede, Ole Johannsen, said indignantly, "Such narrow-mindedness ... no, I'd rather not say anything ... But this will bring forth bad blood ..." Untersturmführer Hessler hedged the same sentiments. But he believed that they should first arm the Ukrainians. Helmut Kolbe thought so too. Only a few, including Otto Schmidt, didn't agree to have the Slavic people armed. Wind came out of northeast during the 28th of December. It got colder and the snowfall worse. A swarm of ravens flew swiftly over the lines. One bird came down all of a sudden, and flew over Xaver's head, crowing excitedly. "Just calm down,"

Xaver yelled back and waved to the raven. "I've understood you — you want to warn me of bad weather ..." Soon, a storm came up and howled past the men's ears, and blew dense flakes of snow over the sweeping fields. The MG, covered with a tarp, was snowed-in in no time. Unterburger busily tried to keep the masses of snow out of his foxhole. Doggedly, he worked his spade during the entire watch. Then it was Heinz Meyer's turn, who almost couldn't find the MG position, because it was difficult to see anything and his calls couldn't be heard above the howling wind. Finally, the wind made a short pause and then he could hear Xaver's answering call. "I'm over here!" He wasn't that far away from the MG position.

Heinz Meyer tromped the last few meters through the dense falling snowflakes and deep snow, which went up to the knees, and came up to the emplacement breathing hard. Panting, he asked, "Anything going on?" "Nothing, except for the snow storm and shoveling snow!" Unterburger answered. "See you later." And off he went to disappear into the howling snowflakes. A few strides later, a heavy gust of wind threw him onto the ground. He could hardly breathe as he got back up, and then another gust blew him down. He had lost his MP and with groping hands he searched for it in the snow. After turning a few rounds, he found it again. He breathed a sigh of relief. The wind had died down a little. Unterburger got up and stomped through the snow. Occasionally, he had to stem himself against the wind. Then he tripped over something and as he bent over to feel what it was, he noticed that it was a solidly frozen body of a Red Army soldier. He knew now that he had gone in the wrong direction. Suddenly, the terrible howling wind came up again and with great force, which knocked him down once again. When he came too, he noticed that it had become stiller. Unterburger sat upright and tried to orientate himself. Which direction should he go? The snowfall wasn't so strong anymore, but still so dense that he couldn't see anything. It was useless to ponder, he must try. He started to fight his way through the snow again. That was hard work and uncomfortable, since he had enough to do to simply keep himself on his feet. He felt he'd rather just lie down in the soft snow and go to sleep.

All of a sudden, he stood before something dark. He went to it and then found himself standing before a destroyed tank. Quickly, a pair of strong hands took a hold of him and threw him down. He defended himself vigorously. He was a strong wrestler and boxer. It was two enemy soldiers who had waylaid him. They didn't use firearms, because they had orders to get a prisoner alive. The weather was ideal for this, because their opponent's visibility and hearing were strongly reduced in the storm. He knocked-out one attacker with a right hook; the other took a knife in his hand. Breathing heavily, Xaver leaned against the tank and awaited the next assault. With a curse on his lips, the enemy soldier lunged forward and threw himself at him. Xaver made a small turn and the attacker slammed his head against the tank's armor, and then he received a hand chop across the back of his neck. Motionless, the attacker lied in the snow. That couldn't have been all there was, Xaver thought and took the MP from his shoulder. He moved carefully with weapon in hand alongside the tank. A shadow suddenly appeared before him. As quick as Lightning, he pulled the trigger. The shadow sank down. The German turned around to check on the other two men and saw that one was moving. Quickly, he went over and sent the man into the land of dreams with the butt of his weapon. The one by the tank was dead and the other lies not far away, shot. Xaver went around the wrecked tank, but couldn't find any other enemy soldiers.

He searched the dead and the live enemy soldiers, but couldn't find any papers on them. Only submachine guns, ammunition, and knives. And now Xaver also knew where he was, because this tank stood about one hundred meters before their positions. Xaver Unterburger sat beside the tank and waited until the unconscious soldier had awakened from his dreams. The snow storm had abated by the time the unconscious man started to move again. Xaver kicked him in his ass, hung the three MPs around his neck, let dangling on his back, and showed him which direction to go. He drove him onwards to the German lines. "Dawai — pasholl!" When they were about fifty steps away from the own lines, he shouted, "Don't shoot — it's me, Unterburger Xaver!" It was snowing only lightly now. Not a sound came from over there. Only when they were about twenty meters before the MG position, which was occupied by Grossert, did a loud voice call out, "Halt! Password!" Angrily, Unterburger yelled, "Shitty password – it's me, Unterburger Xaver! Password is Dora!" "Man, Xaver – where're you coming from? Who is that guy?" "Ask him yourself!" Xaver laughed; he was glad to be back. Kolbe and Schmidt were about to leave to search for Unterburger, when just then he came stomping into the bunker with the prisoner. He reported what had happened, wearing a grin. They were very glad to have him back. Kolbe brought the prisoner to the company command post. The Unter-sturmführer was surprised to learn that the enemy would undertake such an action during the storm.

"That could've meant serious consequences for us. We will get a few more surprises from them yet!" As the messenger Anholzer brought the prisoner back to the battalion command post, the enemy's artillery began to fire at the HKL13) and into the rear areas. Perhaps the Soviets knew about the failed attempt of their special mission and wanted to take revenge in this manner. They didn't cause much damage, however, and thus ceased fire a short while later. The days that led up to the 31 st of December had been quiet ones without anything ex-ceptional happening. The enemy had obviously been convinced that he could not break through the lines here. He tried it further north – and was lucky. The Russians had penetrated the entire front lines of the 256th Infantry Division, despite support from the VIII Air Corps, during the 31st of December.

Russian units had seeped through everywhere, also by the 206th Infantry Division, which soon had neared the end of its fighting capabilities. Through these successful enemy advances during the New Year of 1941, the coherency of the German 9th Army had broken apart west of Stariza. Certain incidents happened within the 256th Infantry Division, which had not yet been observed and were unthought-of in the German Wehrmacht. Exhausted soldiers refused to fight on. They screamed into their officer's faces, "Why don't you beat us to death! It doesn't matter who beats us to death!" Lieutenant General Kauffmann, the th commander of the 256 ID, had gone to the supreme commander of the Army, General Strauß, to report that his division could no longer hold-on to Mologino.

They had a remaining combat strength equal to a regiment. The general reminded Kauffmann of Hitler's order, that the lines must be held, and then ordered him to return to his troops, since that was where he belonged. As it turned out during the afternoon of the 31st of December, the situation by Mogolino wasn't as dire as the commander of the 256th ID had illustrated. Mogolino had been held with the help of combat groups, commanded by determined officers, until the morning of 4th of January 1942. This had restrained strong Soviet forces for days, which allowed the retreat of the corps to be carried out in orderly manner. During New Year's Eve, the first sergeant brought some strong punch and crisp bread to the lines. Like a magician, the Stabsscharführer brought forth other goodies from within the vehicle's tarp; cigarettes, schnapps, newspapers, and mail. At around 2400 hours, Untersturmführer Hessler went around to visit the men on the lines to wish them a happy new year. The young soldiers were happy to hear the wishes from their commander and had wished him the same. Most of these young volunteers looked positively to the coming year ... During New Year's Day, the enemy greeted them with a barrage from every heavy weapon they had. The messenger, Andreas Anholzer, who was just coming back from the battalion command post with a report, was killed when he got hit in the chest by a piece of shrapnel. With a sad tone of voice, Untersturmführer Hessler said to Kolbe, "We're constantly getting fewer. Where's all this going to lead to?"

Just then, came the next bad news; Philipp Leitner got killed by a direct hit into his foxhole. His body was nothing more than a bloody heap. The foxhole was made his grave. It was filled with snow. Kolbe's squad, once again, had one man less. With sadness, the men lowered their heads. Who might be next? Kolbe's squad now had six men. The start of the year 1942 had brought a successful breakthrough for the Soviets between the Waldai Heights and the Volga River in south- westerly direction. The Soviet 29th Army was in the area around Bjelji with its masses. Their objective was Smolensk. This resulted in a large gap with a length of around sixteen kilometers between the German VI Corps in Rshev and the XIII Corps to the left. The commander of the 9th Army, General Model, who had the Division Das Reich under his command, planned to attack into this gap with both corps to close it, encircle the enemy, and then annihilate them. During the 10th of January, the Division Das Reich had fallen back from the Rusa lines as planned, to allow a shortening of the front in the area around Gshatsk. The freed-up division was thus given new and difficult tasks. The Regiment DF marched by foot, going back through Gshatsk to Spask. There, they were loaded-up on a train and brought to Sytshevka, which is 50 kilometers south of Rshev. To the north-west of Sytshevka their sister regiment Deutschland was already deployed, which had arrived there with its own vehicles the day before.

General Model ordered the commander of the Division Das Reich to give away one regiment to the VI Corps, which was deployed by Rshev. The regiment was to take part in the attack west of Rshev that was to close a gap in the front-line, and then to help defend the area of penetration by the Volga River. Only the yet-to-be used Regiment DF was in question for this assignment. The battalion, which had a combat strength equal to a company, was distributed among the houses. Kolbe's squad had been assigned quarters on the perimeter of town. Their living and sleeping quarters was a room, which contained a big stove, a table, benches, and two beds that were shared by an old couple, a young woman, and a child of perhaps five years of age. The Landsers slept on the wooden floor.

The boy was mostly lying on top of the stove and watched the goings-on of the German troops. First, they cleaned their weapons. The water was hot, in the meantime, which meant cleaning their bodies and cracking lice. "That won't help us much," Grossert said. "The bed bugs will bite us instead." The two old people were somewhat in a bad mood. They felt pentup. They had hung a large sheet up by their bed. The young woman with the straw-blond hair was friendly. She got water from the well, two wooden tubs and some firewood. Kolbe gave her a piece of soap and the boy a piece of chocolate. The young woman thanked with a friendly smile. Xaver Unterburger grinned. "Our squad leader is flirting." They ate after they had washedup; cooked canned meat and unthawed bread.

Now the boy could no longer keep himself on the stove. He stood by the table. Meyer told him, "Get yourself a loshka (spoon) and a tarelka (plate), and then you can eat with us." The boy went away and soon returned with his mother, who had several plates and spoons with her for the soldiers. Kolbe made it clear to the woman that they could eat too. Happily, she and her boy sat down at the table and ate. She didn't eat it all, though, because half of what she had left over she brought to the old people. The men wrapped themselves up with their tent-halves and blankets and soon fell asleep. Dawn came up outside. Schmidt and Johannsen had first watch. About an hour later, Schmidt awakened the sleeping men. "Don't worry, we're not going up front again — we're receiving warm food to munch," he said to calm them back down.

"And I thought we're going at it again," Grossert uttered, and was glad that it wasn't so. Grossert and Unterburger took the mess kits that the Russian woman had cleaned and went to get goulash and noodles for the squad at the field kitchen, which was located a few houses away. The cook told them, "You can have as much seconds as you want, and if it is all right with the gentlemen, you can have tea with rum later on." Grossert had the woman give him a large pot and went back to get the so-called seconds for the Russians. Now the old couple was friendly too. Everyone was merry later on, while drinking the tea with rum. Untersturmführer Hessler dropped by with Rottenführer Kirchner, who was a good harmonica player. Hessler had a bottle of Steinhäger with, which made its rounds many times. The Russians also got to drink tea with rum. The young woman put a bowl of sweet and sour pickles on the table and smiled at Kolbe. "She'd like to do something else with you." Hessler grinned as he said that. Kolbe laughed. "First I'd have to get a good sleep." "And when you're all rested it'll be time to march on!" "That is our bitter pill ... One can't change that!" Kolbe frowned with a sweet-sour smile. Berthold Kirchner played Schnadahüpferln. The young Landsers joined-in with the singing. "Es ist halt mein Vater sein einziger Trost, Holladeri-Holladero, das ihm solang er mich hat, sein Geld nicht verrost', Holladeri-Holladero, schneid's o..."

The next day a number of replacements were allocated. Kolbe's squad also received a new man. He stemmed from Graz. Sepp Achleitner was a carpenter. Kolbe had a job for him right away. He had him saw and chop fire wood, which was stacked behind the house – to keep him from getting out of practice, the squad leader said. The restful days had brought Kolbe and the young Russian woman closer together. She called him Sepp and he called her Masha. The Landsers smiled with sympathy. Let the Unterscharführer have delight with the pretty young woman. Who knew if he could ever hold a woman in his arms again? The next fighting could change everything. Then it was time; the next assignment had been given. By train they were taken back to Rshev. It was not easy to say their goodbyes for Kolbe and Masha. Masha leaned against him and cried and because she cried so did the lad. Even the old babushka shed a few tears. The overall combat strength of the Regiment DF was very low; two battalions that had two companies each and the leftovers of an MG company. The field howitzer company had one light and one heavy platoon; two platoons with 37mm Pak. These units along with the staff and communications, made all together 650 men! The Regiment DF had the assignment to reach a sharp turn on the Volga River to the north- west of Rshev, and to prepare for defense on both sides of the river, facing northeast, along a length of about 6 kilometers. At the same time, other units were to defend in the own rear area to the south-west against the encircled enemy.

Along the way, the Regiment DF was forced to fight along certain segments of the roadway, leading from Sytchevka to Rshev, to clear them from the enemy. In practically the last minute had the regiment arrived Rshev on the 25th of January. The battalions, in which the leftovers of the 15th and 16th Companies had been distributed, were thrown into battle without delay. "Well then let's go men! Good luck!" the Untersturmführer called out to his men. The attack to the north-west went smoothly. The enemy was offering only weak resistance; the regiment arrived on the Volga even before noontime on the 25th of January. The regimental commander, Obersturmbannführer (colonel) Kumm, together with the commander of the 1st Battalion, Sturmbannführer Ehrath, and the commander of the 3rd Battalion, Hauptsturmführer (capatain) Schulz, had determined the main line of defense. The 1st Battalion was deployed on the western side of the river, and the 3rd Battalion on the eastern side. The Volga had such a thick layer of ice that it could even support heavy tanks. A small settlement, called Klepenino with maybe thirty houses, was situated on the eastern side, where the 3rd Battalion was. The terrain east of the place was wide and open with low rolling hills. A forest was situated about eighty meters from the border of the village and where the main defensive-line ran, and formed a point towards the north-east. A small wood with a breadth of around 600 meters was situated behind the battalion. The 1st Battalion had better defensive features. Here, the main line of defense ran about 200 meters to the north of a forest and had a good field of fire.

The view over the fore field was good. The Landsers had dug deep holes into the deep snow. The Pioniers had blown holes into the solid frozen ground with special charges and landmines. The MG positions were placed about two to three hundred meters apart along with foxholes. All together a rather thin defensive line that had no depth to it. But the young volunteers were used to such shenanigans, as they called these situations. They knew that their regiment had no reserves. With permission of the regimental commander, Kumm, the commander of the 3rd Battalion, Hauptsturmführer Schulz decided to penetrate the forest, which lay before his positions, to move his lines to the north of the wood. The battalion commander wanted to at least have outposts stationed there. The battalion attacked and was surprised to find good defensive emplacements there, which were partially inside dense brushwork and hedges. It was an older Soviet defensive system, which stemmed from the fighting during the fall. Without stopping, the Landsers fought their way through the dense bush. Their snow shirts got ripped open and they injured their faces as they fired from the hips against an enemy who defended himself stubbornly. The sounds of shooting and exploding hand grenades echoed throughout the forest. Despite having bullets flying sharply past their ears, the Landsers doggedly pressed-on the charge. They didn't avoid hand-to-hand fighting either. They charged the enemy, going over the dead and wounded. Just gain ground!

As the bitter fighting went back and forth, the enemy's superiority grew. Sepp Achleitner, who was fighting for the first time, came upon two enemy soldiers who had no more ammo and were charging him with raised rifles. He managed to shoot one of them, but the second had whacked him over his shoulder and the blow threw him down onto the ground. Just as the Red Army soldier lifted his rifle to strike him a second time, a submachine gun garb brought him down. Kolbe knelt down beside Achleitner and helped him to get up. While his face grimaced in pain, he followed Kolbe. He gasped for air, his knees were wobbly, and the shoulder throbbed. He hadn't imagined war to be this way. He had killed a human being, saw into his eyes, real close ... Hauptsturmführer Schulz had determined that the attack against such an over-powering opponent, who had been receiving rein-forcements during the fight, was hopeless. He called-off the attack and ordered the men to return to their positions. To assure a retreat with as little casualties as possible, he showed exceptional commitment and fell in the midst of his men. They recovered his dead body and brought it back with them. To replace the popular Hauptsturmführer Schulz, Hauptsturmführer Bollert, who had com-manded the 10th Company, took over the 3rd Bat-talion. The enemy took advantage of the situation and pressed-on their own attack, but was stopped before the German lines and, as they retreated back into the forest with shots fired after them, they suffered high losses.

The battalion too had suffered painful losses. Kolbe's squad lost Achleitner, due to a suspected broken collarbone. Ole Johannsen, Kurt Grossert, and Heinz Meyer were lightly wounded through grazing shots. The battalion command post was situated about eight hundred meters behind the lines of the 3rd Battalion in a small village, which was around fifty meters south of a forest. General Model came here every day, because he had determined that this sector was especially endangered. Once, he showed-up with a Fieseler Storch, another time by car, and some-times even on a horse. On the 28th of January, just as General Model was visiting the regiment, a prisoner was brought in, who had been a radio man with the staff of the Soviet 39th Army. Such captives were rare and they sometimes knew more

than some commanders. The Russian was very talk-
ative. He told them that a major attack was planned
for the next day. The goal was to punch through
the lines to allow the encircled Soviet crops to be
freed. For this purpose, they had the entire 39th
Army standing in rank and file along the road
leading from Kalinin through Wassikoje all the way
to the great bend on the Volga; seven rifle divisions
and six tank brigades. They were to carry-on the
attacks, initiated by the 29th Army. General Model
left the command post full of worries. He warned
his men to be of utmost alert, even though he knew
this warning had not been necessary with these
experienced men. "Obersturmbannführer," Model said
to Kumm. "I'm counting on you." Smiling, he added,

"But perhaps the Ivan in there told us a tall tale."
The regiment was put on top alert that late afternoon. Each and every Landser had been told what
the enemy had planned. Whoever had the oppor-
tunity, wrote a letter to their parents at home, so
that the first sergeant could pick them up later,
when he came to bring food and ammunition after
nightfall. Untersturmführer Hessler went from man
to man. "Be brave, men. We've overcome a lot and
will master the coming too..." Otto Schmidt and Ole
Johannsen were in their MG nest and stared out
over towards the forest. It was eerily still. If it
weren't for the dead, lying in the fore field, there
would otherwise be nothing there to remind one
that a war was going on. Schmidt broke the quiet
spell. "Aren't you going to write ...?" "How could
I? You can't even take off your gloves in this

damned cold!" It was more than minus forty degrees! Every soldier had fastened a small stick on his mitten, to allow pulling the trigger with it instead of the trigger finger. The exposed finger would otherwise freeze, and even regular gloves were of little help in this grim cold. Shortly before mid-night, food and ammunition had been brought up front. The men also received incendiaries and mines for combating the tanks. In addition to this, the first sergeant had also brought bundled stick grenades. A few replacements too had come with. Albert Schoemaker was among them. He had been a member of Kolbe's squad and stemmed from Flanders.

He was wounded in September, and now he got to be with his old squad again. When Untersturmführer Hessler had asked him what the people back in Flanders were saying about the war with the Soviet Union, Albrecht Schoemaker answered; "It is better that we are here, than the Russians in Flanders." "Go to your squad. We're expecting some heavy fighting. Good luck!" said the company commander. "Thank you, Untersturmführer. I wish you good luck too!" "It's nice that you're coming!" Kolbe called out cheerfully. "Thank you, Unterscharführer. I'm glad to see that you're well!" Kolbe told him to leave out the polite form of you and to use the informal you, since everyone did so. "You can call me Sepp!" "Yes, Unter ... err ... Sepp!" The Russians commenced the dawn of the 29th of January with a heavy bombardment. Volleys from Stalin organs joined in. The air was filled with non-stop whistling, hissing, and howling of the enemy's projectiles. A cloud of snow dust and powder gasses hovered in the air over the positions of the Regiment DF. The Landsers cowered deeply in their foxholes and clenched their teeth. They were inundated with snow and icy chunks of dirt. Then the attackers poured out of the forest, supported by tanks whose tracks spewed-up clouds of snow. They didn't have it far to the 3rd Battalion's defensive position, only about eighty meters. "Fire!" the company commander Hessler shouted with a piercing voice. All at once the Germans started to fire from their thinly occupied lines.

The enemy's front ranks tumbled into the snow, as if a scythe had cut them down. Now the German's own field howitzer fired with high-explosive shells into the masses of attackers. Several tanks were destroyed in short order by an **88**mm Flak and a 5cm Pak. The Landsers fired until the barrels steamed. The MGs didn't need to have their barrels changed so often in this cold. It depended on the length of the battle. The enemy's attack began to diminish. The shrill battle cry "Uraah" started to wane. Most of the tanks had stopped, and only a few dared to carry on the attack. They didn't make it far before the Flak or a Pak got them. But the forest kept on spitting out more masses of attackers, and the officers and commissars drove on the Red Army troops to attack with shouts and threats. The newcomers pushed the ones who were lagging behind to go onward. Otto Schmidt was lying behind his machine gun, breathing hard with anxiety. "Hot damn, who is supposed to shoot all of them?" he hollered." I hope we have enough ammo." "It's enough to send whole masses into hell ... And now fire, they're coming again!" Ole Johannsen shouted agitated. The dance of death went on. Now First lieutenant Tisemeyer's battery, which stood not far from the regimental command post, got involved in the fight. The lead-gray air was filled with whining and howling. The shells detonated with thunderous clash and lightning amongst the attackers, which kept getting closer to the lines, despite heavy losses. At least the tanks were kept at bay by the Flak and the Pak platoon. Once again, burning and smoldering tanks stood before the German lines.

A few had their turrets blown off when their own ammunition exploded within. Now that their tanks couldn't advance, the Red Army soldiers tried a trick, in order to get into the battalion's lines. They crept through the deep snow towards the recognized MG nests and foxholes, while their tanks kept a concentrated fire at the Germans. A shell whistled at hair's breadth over Grossert's MG position and exploded barely three meters behind it. Startled, Grossert and Meyer ducked down low inside their foxhole. Meyer pulled the machine gun inside quick as lightning. "They've spotted us," he said grimly. "Now only heaven can help us." It was a Pak that got the T-26 between the turret and the chassis. The tank jolted backwards a bit, and then the driver's hatch opened, from which a figure came out and dropped into the snow. A thunderous bang followed immediately afterwards, and then the tank was engulfed in flames. "Watch out!" cried Kolbe. "The Ivans are crawling through the snow!" And then he fired a burst from his MP. The enemy had approached to within forty meters in front of Schmidt's MG position. Schmidt fired and small geysers sprouted up from the snow. Johannsen threw hand grenades. They detonated with a dull sound. With shouts, a few enemy soldiers sprung out of the snow, got hit by the garbs from the MG and were thrown back into the snow, where they remained, bleeding. Two or three enemy hand grenades exploded before Grossert's MG position. He yanked the machine gun up. Meyer threw a hand grenade into a track in the snow.

Grossert fired the MG and scored a hit. An enemy soldier jumped up, cried with pain, and then sunk back down. Even though many had been spotted in time, a few still managed to get close to the lines and remained there quietly. The battalion commander crawled up to the company command post, situated on the northern outskirts of Klepenino, during the afternoon. "How's it going!" he asked Untersturmführer Hessler. "Good, up until now. And when the Pak and Flak keep the tanks away from us, then no one will get through!" Hessler said determined. "The question is how long they want to keep at it." The battalion commander sighed. "They seem to have all the trumps ... if this should go on day and night, we won't be able to hold. Without a few hours of sleep the men will get exhausted. We desperately need back-up. The regiment commander had requested reinforcements several times. Where can you get them without stealing? The army wants us to hold, cost it what it may." "The price may be very high!" Untersturmführer Hessler growled. "We are expected to achieve the highest commitment. The final soldiery consequence is each soldier's life, as sacrifice for a cause that should be in everyone's heart. Otherwise, he couldn't be so dedicated to accomplish this," said Hauptsturmführer Bollert. Then he said goodbye. Hessler hadn't even mentally digested the battalion commander's words yet, when the Soviets started to attack again. The breakthrough to free the surrounded corps must be accomplished, may it cost what it will.

That was the enemy's motto. They kept charging against the thin lines of the Regiment DF without pause. The enemy threw regiment after regiment, battalion after battalion, and finally brigades into the battle. But he made a great tactical mistake; those forces weren't put to use to achieve a breakthrough, because they failed to set a point of main effort. The men of the Regiment DF bitterly held on to their positions. They did not yield, even when their strength was overstrained. Each man's achievement, here before Klepenino, had gone far beyond what had been done before. Every charge by the enemy had been repulsed with terribly high losses for him, mostly through close-quarter fighting with hand grenades and spades. The dead enemy soldiers grew to piles before Klepenino. The men of the Regiment DF would have never been able to hold had it not been for the thirteen Pak of the Panzer-Jäger-Abteilung 561 (tank destroyer battalion) from the regular army. The two tank destroyer platoons, under the command of Lieutenant Petermann, had destroyed twenty enemy tanks by the 3rd of February. The enemy's major assault had waned by the 4th of February. The enemy seemed to have exhausted himself. It got a little warmer and eventually it started to snow. The tired Landsers breathed a sigh of relief. They oiled their MG and MP receivers between bites of crisp bread and snow, and also got their positions squared away. The lightly wounded men, who could not fight anymore, drug their seriously wounded comrades back into Klepenino.

There, they awaited nightfall, when the medics would come with horse drawn sleds to bring them to the main aid station. Those of which who could walk didn't wait for darkness; they went to the aid station right away while supporting each other. It happened time and again that they would have to take cover from the enemy's harassing fire and even got wounded a second time by shrapnel. A few never reached the main aid station, others only as dead men. It was a gruesome tragedy! Heinz Meyer, from Brandner's squad, was making his torturous way to the rear. He had received a piece of shrapnel in his right shoulder. A comrade behind him collapsed from exhaustion. Moaning, he lied in the snow with bloody foam on his lips. Heinz Meyer and another comrade wanted to help him up, but the wounded man waved them off. A gush of blood ran down his chin. He gasped as he stretched- out, his eyes widened, and then he died. Meyer closed the man's eyes. He took his valuables, the one half of his dog-tag, and his identification and pay book- let. Then he went on, hobbled with the others in silence. Another wounded comrade moaned behind Meyer "Why? This damned shit!" Exhausted, the wounded troop had arrived at the main aid station six kilometers away in Nashkino. There they re- ceived treatment from military doctors, who were resolutely helping the wounded. Then the wounded men yearningly wait to be transported further on to a military hospital.

The enemy attacked again on the 3rd of February with great force. The fighting was especially hard before Klepenino, against an enemy who was far superior in numbers. The crew of an anti-tank gun, stationed before the village, had to be replaced three times within a few hours. The commander of the anti-tank platoon, Lieutenant Petermann got wounded. Lieutenant Hofer took-over command for him. There stood twenty four Soviet tank wrecks before the lines of the Regiment DF - and the bitter fighting went on. The far outnumbered Landsers fought in desperation. They defended their positions like berserkers, allowed the tanks to roll over their foxholes and kept the enemy infantry at bay. The masses of dead lying before the German lines increased to an unbearable extend. And this madness went on! One crew of a 37mm Pak stayed at their gun until the last moment, when a T-34 shot them up and then rolled over them. Then the colossus went about to enter the ruined village. As Kolbe emerged from a ruined house's cellar with two boxes of MG ammo for Grossert's machine gun, he saw how a Landser got cut down with a tank's on-board machine gun twenty meters before the vehicle, which the soldier had attempted to destroy with a mine. He wasn't in the tank's blind spot yet, Kolbe thought and set the ammo boxes down. The tank approached carefully and he hadn't discovered Kolbe yet. A jolt went through the Unterscharführer. Now! He sprung up and ran, took the mine out of the dead Landser's hand and threw it underneath the right track. Quick as lightning, he sought cover within some ruins.

A short moment later it seemed as if the world had ended. To him the explosion wasn't simply a noise, but a thunderous roar. For a few winks of an eye, he went unconscious. When he came-to, he saw through smoke and snow mist that the tank stood askew to the house ruins. Then he saw the turret and driver's hatches opening. Two heads appeared, donning leather helmets. As they attempted to exit the tank, their bodies jerked before they dropped back inside. Kolbe heard nothing. He did not notice Untersturmführer Hessler shouting at him, "Give me cover!" He saw Hessler drop a bundle charge into the driver's hatch and then taking cover beside him. There was another thunderous blast. Dark, oily smoke billowed out of the hatches. The tank will explode soon. Got to get away! Hessler grabbed Kolbe's arm. "Get away!" he shouted into his ear.

Kolbe understood. He grabbed the ammo boxes and in a crouch he ran to Grossert's MG position, going around the smoldering tank in a half-circle. Hessler followed him, but didn't make it to the position. Just before reaching it, he got hit by a shot that went through his lower left arm. The wound bled badly. Kolbe helped Hessler to go back to the village outskirts. Behind a timbered wall he wrapped a leather strap around his arm to stop the bleeding. Then he bandaged the wound. "Shit!" said Kolbe. "Paul, that's a breaking- shot. The bone is splintered. You must go back immediately!" Hessler's face grimaced with pain. "Sepp, you take over the company. I'm going to the main aid station. I can make it. Go back to the men!" "Later, Rudi! We're going to miss you a lot ..." Kolbe uttered and then ran to get back to the fighting. "Bye, Sepp - get through in one piece!" the Untersturmführer called after him.

In the night, Kolbe snuck along the company's positions. Twenty three men were holding a line that was over one kilometer long! They haven't slept for nights and hadn't received any warm food either. They've reached the end of their strength, both physically and mentally. The machine gunner I, Sturmmann Otto Schmidt, was now a squad leader, and his squad had four men. Albert Schoemaker had been taken out, because his toes were frozen. Along with Schmidt, there were only Kurt Grossert, Ole Johannsen, and Xaver Unterburger in the squad. The men greatly regretted that Hessler was no longer with them. The enemy attacked their positions once again shortly before midnight, without the support of artillery and tanks. It was their misfortune that the winds had dissipated the cloud-cover and that the Germans were alert. Their assault was bloodily repulsed, despite the enemy's use of tank wrecks and their dead comrades for cover. Thirty light tanks appeared before the 10th Company's positions the next day, and had advanced to fifty meters of the foxholes. Then they opened fire with all weapons and sent a fusillade of bullets at the MG nests and foxholes. A half hour later they disappeared back into the forest. Had the enemy known that the Pak couldn't change positions because the crews had no vehicles available to them? Biting cold covered the snowy fields – and silence. No one moved! Two hours after the attack, the only survivor, Rottenführer Wagner, crawled through the deep snow.

Badly wounded and with frozen hands, he was found and brought to the battalion command post. With his last bit of strength he attempted to stand at attention before the commander of the 3rd Battalion, Hauptsturmführer Bollert. But he collapsed. While lying down, he reported; "Hauptsturmführer, I'm the last survivor of the company! All the other comrades have fallen!" He stretched-out and then closed his eyes forever. Now, no one was left from the 10th Company ... Quickly, the VI Army Corps filled the one thousand meter gap with one hundred and twenty men; they were cobblers, tailors, drivers, cooks, and were led by quartermasters. None had combat experience. They had barely occupied the former 10th Company's positions, when the Russians bombarded them with mortars, which was a terrible thing for the men from the rear echelon. Then the Russians attacked, shouting their guttural and shrill sounding battle cry, "Uraah." This had caused the men's nerves to falter all together. They made a deadly mistake. They began to flee and were shot from behind. For sure, these troops from the rear detachments were honorable men, but totally inexperienced and not able to carry on a fight, and especially under such extreme conditions! That night it was possible for the enemy to get through the gap and appeared the following morning from out of the forest with strong infantry and tank forces fifty meters before the regiment command post. In anticipation to such an event, a few houses along the edge of the settlement had been prepared for defense.

The flooring had been torn out, deep holes dug and embrasures were put into the lower wooden walls. Every man, be it driver, radio operator, or messenger, was put to use to help hold the sector. The commander of the Regiment DF, Obersturmbannführer Kumm, who had requested the VI Corps to send reserves, now strongly demanded these to help change the unbearable conditions. The commander's perception of the situation had found no acceptance as truth there. Only the half hour visit at the regiment's command post by the chief of staff of the VI Corps had persuaded them of the regiment's dire situation. The Soviet attacks had been stopped fifteen meters before the houses of Klepenino. There, the dead lay. The corps sent an infantry regiment, which consisted of two weak battalions, for assistance. This regiment was supposed to push the enemy back through the forest and over the main defensive line and then link-up there with the 3rd Battalion of the DF Regiment. However, the regiment's attack was ill-fated. The battalions had barely penetrated into the forest when they were beaten back with bloody losses during a counterattack by the enemy. The battalion commanders and officers had a difficult task to roundup the badly decimated companies again. It was out of the question to attempt another attack and hope for success. The rest of the inftantry regiment had been integrated with the battalions of DF, or were used to cover the flanks, and the commander was called back to the corps. During all of this, the 1st and 3rd Battalions were incessantly attacked frontally.

The enemy broke through with a battalion by the 2nd Company during the night of the 8th of February. Bitter close quarter fighting ensued, by which the company, which had the strength of a platoon, was completely annihilated. Not a single German soldier had survived the slaughter! The casualties that the 3rd Battalion suffered through death, wounded, and freezing were so high that the rest of the men, there were nine (!), were put into the 1 st Battalion. The village of Klepenino, whose houses had all been destroyed, was evacuated. The defensive positions of the 1 st Battalion were taken back to where the battalion command post was. Of Untersturmführer's Hessler's company, there were only Unterscharführer Kolbe, Rottenführer Kirchner and the Swede, Ole Johannsen left over. Kurt Grossert fell when he attacked an enemy tank. Otto Schmidt got wounded on his upper right arm during an enemy attack, and Xaver Unterburger had lost three fingers of his right hand through frostbite. Now the enemy attacked the new lines without interruption. Their artillery fire got stronger by the day. The Landsers cowered in their snow holes in the grim cold and fended off all attacks with curses on their lips. Helmut Kolbe, Berthold Kirchner and Ole Johannsen lie along a line fifty to sixty meters apart. Kirchner was operating an MG-34 and his second machine gunner was a young infantryman from the regular army. The boy stemmed from Mecklenburg and his name was Jörg Hansen. He barely understood Kolbe's Tyrolean dialect, but he knew what had to be done.

"And this is right!" Kirchner said with his specific vernacular. In these times of greatest need, the Regiment DF received useable reinforcements: a reconnaissance battalion from the army under the command of Major Mummert, who was an excellent officer, and a motorcycle battalion from the Division Das Reich under command of Hauptsturmführer Tychsen. The Aufklärungs-Abteilung 14 (AA 14 – reconnaissance battalion14) took over the positions of the regiment staff, so that at least a continuous running front-line could be established. Around the 11 th to 12th of February, the enemy succeeded in breaking through the solid line formed by the infantry battalion. The Soviets crossed over the ice of the Volga and with strong forces they occupied a small strip of woods on the western shoreline (Volga bend). This wood went down in the regiment's history as the "Russian Woods". Additional badly needed reinforcements had arrived: portions of the Sturmgeschütz Abteilung (assault gun battalion) 189. In addition, a mortar unit with 210mm mortars had taken the "Russian Woods" under fire and had caused a bloodbath among the densely packed enemy troops. Despite the combined attacks by the AA 14 under Major Kummert and the motorcycle battalion under Hauptsturmführer Tychsen, only by the eleventh try -- after the woods had changed hands ten times -- was it possible to take and keep possession of the "Russian Woods". The Red Army troops had literally defended themselves down to the last drop of blood and the last bullet!

Despite the Herculean exertions, the fighting spirit of the remaining small number of men of the Regiment "Der Führer" was unbroken. They stayed in their thinly manned positions. During the 16th of February the Soviets went at it again. After a bombardment from every caliber of artillery they had available, and with the support of ten tanks, they went forward in battalion strength against the very weakly occupied defensive line, held by the small rest of the Regiment DF. The young infantryman, Jörg Hansen, believed to be in hell. He had never been through anything like this before. He pressed himself hard against the ground and clenched his teeth together. The air was full of infernal howling and screeching. The nasty smell of powder gasses irritated the mucus, making one to cough, and the frozen ground droned from the detonating shells. Finally, the terrible ruckus had relented some, the snow-clouds dissipated, and the enemy's artillery wandered to the rear. Bertl Kirchner lifted his head and elbowed the boy. "Got weak nerves?" he shouted. Hansen looked-up. "I'm ready!" he declared determined. But when he saw what was approaching, he momentarily closed his eyes. "We'll shoot only at the Ivans. The tanks we will avoid - let the Pak take care of them. Keep with me, and everything will be alright!" Kirchner wasn't usually like that, but he liked the boy. They didn't have to evade the tanks, because the boom of cannon fire of the Sturmgeschütze came from the forest's edge, and they had destroyed three enemy tanks within minutes with their anti-tank rounds.

The Red Army troops jumped off the vehicles, shouting. The tanks stood in the snow smoldering. The rest of the tanks halted and fired what they could into the forest. The answer came straight away. Two other tanks got hit and started to burn. Now, five tanks were in flames. With loud noise, the onboard ammunition exploded and blew off the turrets. The rest of the tanks carefully moved forward. With lots of shouting, the officers and commissars formed their companies for the attack. The destroyed tanks were a shock for the Red Army soldiers, who'd rather run the other way. Now they came, however. The threats they had received by their superiors had been effective. When the attackers were to within one hundred meters, the defenders opened fire all at once. Whole bundles of troops, who had bunched together out of fear, got hit and dropped into the snow. The Sturmgeschütz had, in the meantime, destroyed two more tanks. The other three tanks were not to be held back anymore. They began to flee. The Red Army soldiers joined them. All threats were to no avail. Even though a few were killed, the troops fled. Then something outrageous happened. The Soviet artillery put up a massive curtain of fire before the own fleeing soldiers and forced them to turn around to continue the attack! The eighth tank was now burning. The other two gave their attacking comrades fire support. Then, with full throttle, they went charging through the German defensive lines and disappeared into the woods The remainders of the attackers, now left alone, were stopped fifty meters before the German defensive positions.

Their hoarse battle cry, "Uraah", had fallen silent. Now the Sturmgeschütze began to fire into the ranks of the enemy infantry with high-explosive shells. If the enemy soldiers went back, they would get shot as cowards, if they went forward, they would die as heroes ... Well then - attack! With desperate courage, they stormed while shouting. A few made it to fifteen meters before the Germans before they sink bleeding into the snow. A few threw hand grenades with success. Kirchner got wounded by shrapnel on his right cheek and upper arm. "Dammit!" he ranted. "Throw a few eggs into that nest up ahead! But count, or else they'll come flyin' back!" Jörg Hansen prepared three egg hand

grenades, pulled the fuse, counted, and then threw
-- he did this three times in succession. Boom!
Boom! Boom! Not a single Red Army soldier was
moving anymore. Only a few badly wounded men
could be heard moaning. Otherwise, it was still.
Jörg Hansen wrapped bandages on Kirchner. The
wounds didn't bleed much. "Don't you worry, Jörg,
I'm stayin' here!" he said when Hansen looked ques-
tionably at him. After dark, Kolbe came sneaking.
"Come on, Bertl; let's get some food and some ammo
for our MPs." "Take the Swede with you -- I can't!"
Kirchner told him about his wounds, and that he
didn't want to go to the main aid station.

After a while, Kolbe returned, accompanied by Ole
Johannsen. Both dragged along captured rucksacks.
They left one with Kirchner and Hansen. It contained some crumbs of millet bread, bacon,
machorka, and two drums of submachine gun ammo.
They had also brought a Russian MP for Hansen.
Kirchner explained how it functioned. "There isn't
anyone left alive out there," Kolbe told them. "Ac-
tually, I feel sorry for those poor dogs." On the
17th of February, it was announced that the battle
was over. The Soviet 29th Army and a large
portion of the 39th didn't exist anymore. General
Model, who had been the supreme commander of the
9th Army since the 1st of February, had forced a
turnaround with his divisions in this middle section
of the German eastern front. The Regiment Der
Führer was replaced on the lines by an army division on the 18th of February. Proudly, the rest

of the men marched back to the divisional head-quarters. As Obersturmbannführer Otto Kumm went to report at the headquarters of the Division Das Reich, General Model also happened to be there. "I know what your regiment went through, Kumm," he said. "But I can't grasp it yet. What is its re-maining strength?" "General, sir, my regiment is outside in formation!" The general looked out the window. Outside stood thirty five men! The Regi-ment Der Führer, which went well beyond the call of duty during this deployment, had played a deci-sive role in helping to stabilize the Army Group Center's frontlines.

During these weeks, the enemy had suffered 15,000 casualties before the regiment's sector. And in this same time, over 70 enemy tanks had been destroyed, partially through close quarter methods. Alas, the regiment had to endure severe losses. From the total strength of 650 men at the beginning, 150 had fallen, 465 got wounded or were out of action through frostbite. The Regiment "Der Führer" was reorganized into a Panzergrenadier-Regiment in mid March 1942.

END

Dear Reader,

My name is Friedrich von Gatow, the author of "Stahlgewitter – at the gates of Moscow" and "Helden der Ostfront". I hope you like my work and that you enjoyed reading my book. I am retired and writing my books in my free time. I hope to give you a good time.

My father experienced some episodes of the book exactly as described. Some passages of my books were created in my imagination, some based on memoirs of the front fighters. I dedicate my series of books to him and the many nameless veterans of his generation.

I have no support from a publisher or editors. Criticism is part of learning, improving and success. For me, criticism is a motivation to improve. That's why, please support me with your feedback. Please take 5 minutes time and write a review at amazon. It is the only way for me how to get your feedback. I donate half of the proceeds from the book series to "Volksbund deutscher Kriegsgräberfürsorge e.V." (War Memorial Care) and for wounded veterans who fought in Afghanistan (Kriegsopferfürsorge)

Thank you for your attention – Walter Mönch!

Bibliography

Dokumente der Deutschen Politik und Geschichte von 1848 bis zur Gegenwart. Bd. 5: Die Zeit der nationalsozialistischen Diktatur 1933-1945, Il, Teil: Deutschland im Zweiten Weltkrieg 1939-1945. Hg. v. K. Hohlfeld, Berlin 0. J. (zit.:DDPG)

H.G.Dahms: Geschichte des Zweiten Weltkrieges

Joachim C. Fest: Das Gesicht des Dritten Reiches

‚Akten zur deutschen Auswärtigen Politik 1918 bis 1945. Aus dem Archiv des Auswärtigen Amtes; Serie D (1937-1945), Bd. I bis VII, Baden-Baden ff. (zit.: AdAP)

W. Hofer: Die Entfesselung des Zweiten Weltkrieges. Frankfurt a. Main 1960 (zit.: Hofer)

W. Hubatsch: Hitlers Weisungen für die Kriegsführung 1939-1945. Dokumente des Oberkommandos der Wehrmacht, Frankfurt a. M.

Hitler: Reden und Proklamationen 1932-1945. Hg. v.M. Damarus; Bd.1 (1932-1938), Würzburg (zit.: Hitler: Reden u. Proklamationen)

Documents on International Affairs 1939-1946, Vol. II. Hitler's Europe, selected and edited by M. Carlyle, issued under the auspices of the Royal Institute of International Affairs. London, New York, Toronto 1954 (zit.: DIA)

Made in the USA
Coppell, TX
07 May 2020